CHAS WILLIAMSON
Seeking Series: Book Four

SEEKING
the Pearl

Print ISBN: 978-1-949150-29-2

eBook ISBN: 978-1-949150-32-2

Year of the Book

135 Glen Avenue

Glen Rock, PA 17327

Dedication

This book is dedicated to my best friend, soul mate and wife. I am who I am because of you. Your love, kindness, caring, and belief in me allowed me to unleash my potential, to achieve my dreams. Know every heroine's lovable qualities, every good thing about love and relationships in my books are founded in you. You taught me about true love. No character I could ever dream up could ever hold a candle to you. With you by my side, we can do anything. This wonderful life we've lived is because of you. And in my eyes, you are perfect, in every way. My love for you grows exponentially, every day.

When my eyes grow dim and see no more, when my heart stops beating, know this. I will love you forever. You were always there, even before we met. And when we cross over to the other side, our love will always be there, growing stronger every second, way past when eternity is no more. My love for you grows every day, but is as fresh as the day I first saw you. Even after all these years, when I see you, my heart leaps and I feel just like I did the first time you told me you loved me. My heart pounds, my arms tingle and in my chest, my entire being is filled with the warmth of love for you. When nothing is left of the universe, our love will remain, forever and always.

Acknowledgments

To God, for giving me dreams, a wild imagination and for letting me marry my best friend.

To my wife, for being my rock, my love and for encouraging me to make my dreams a reality.

To Travis and Sarah, for supporting your dad's crazy dreams.

To Demi, editor, publisher, friend, for your teaching, guidance and encouragement.

To my Beta readers, Janet, Jackie and Connie for all your help.

To my brother Ronald and my father, Charles Edward Williamson, Jr., for giving me the love of the sea.

Chapter 1

Ellie was ripped from her sleep by the sudden violent movement of the aircraft. Her heartbeat sounded like a kettle drum when she realized the oxygen masks had deployed from overhead. A brilliant white light illuminated the wing outside the window. After she put on the mask, she realized the engine was on fire. Fear ran down the back of her throat, filling the pit of her stomach.

The voice of the stewardess was rapid and high-pitched. "All passengers return to your seats. The captain has turned on the fasten seatbelt sign. Tray tables and seat backs should be returned to their upright position."

The flames were now evident to everyone, orange as they trailed the engine. Some passengers around her were crying, others prayed out loud. Some jerk in the back screamed, "We're all going to die!"

The calm voice of the pilot came overhead. "Ladies and gentlemen, attention please. We appear to have struck something which took out our starboard engine. We will be making an unscheduled stop at the nearest air field. Please remain calm. We will drop altitude rapidly over the next few minutes. Please remain calm. Stewardesses, buckle up. *Now.*"

The cabin lights went off, but Ellie could feel the nose dip forward. *God, please help us.* Loose items rocketed past her in the dark. Something brushed against her shoulder. She realized it was the oxygen mask from the seat row behind her. The plane was going straight down. *Please God, no!*

The captain must have forgotten to turn off the intercom because a voice filled the cabin. "May Day, May Day. This is flight two-one-niner-niner declaring an in-flight emergency. Something has struck our aircraft. Fire in starboard engine. Appear to have lost all controls on starboard wing. Loss of pressure in braking system. Cabin pressure's dropping. Request emergency clearance for landing..."

The cabin was suddenly quiet. The silence was deafening. Ellie had to brace her arms on the seat in front of her to stay in place. How could everyone be so calm? Ellie looked around and realized there were no other passengers, just her. *Did the rapture occur and You forgot me?*

The terrifying rollercoaster ride abruptly flattened out. The hum of landing gear being lowered filled the cabin along with the thump of wheels locking in place. The motion vibrated through the airframe. Ellie looked out her window. A tall mountain was directly in her view and growing larger.

The intercom once again sprang to life with the voice of a stewardess. "Everyone assume brace positions. Put your head down and hug your knees. If you can't, cradle your head against the seat back in front of you. Now, brace, brace, brace. Brace, brace, brace."

Ellie lost it. She opened her mouth to scream, but nothing came out. Hands were on her arms, shaking her.

"Ellie, wake up. We're making the final approach into Heathrow."

Panicked, she saw Jeremy's smiling face.

"But the plane... What did we hit?"

"Hit? Nothing. Flight's been as smooth as cream. You okay?"

Her breath came in clustered rasps. "Must have been a nightmare. I was on the plane when we..."

Jeremy squeezed her hand. "It was a bad dream. Everything's fine. The pilot just put the wheels down. We're almost on the ground."

She closed her eyes and struggled to find peace. Memories of Cleveland on that icy New Year's Day...

"It's all right, Ellie," Jeremy assured her. "It'll be an easy landing, just wait and see." And Jeremy was right. The pilot set the Airbus down gently on the runway. Before long, they'd taxied to the gate. Jeremy retrieved her luggage for her. The worst thing was getting through Immigration, especially since both of them had work visas. After an hour delay, they finally headed to the rental cars. A Land Rover was waiting for them. By 1:00 P.M., they were parked near Trafalgar Square.

"Ready for real fish and chips and mushy peas? Hope you're hungry."

After lunch, they reached the Optimum, the large hotel her employer, GDC, was preparing to open for their client. It would take several months. The hotel had been in bankruptcy when their client acquired it. The intended clientele would be the very rich and famous.

Jeremy's staff had worked day and night on security preparations for the past three months. She and her Aunt Kaitlin had planned her duties to a 'T'. Over the next four months, Ellie would conduct interviews and hire staff. At Ellie's direction, the upscale hotel would equip itself with a five-star staff to cater to their clients' every need.

As the pair approached the hotel, her fish and chips weren't sitting too well. "I don't feel so good, Uncle Jeremy."

"Just your nerves, kiddo. And don't call me 'Uncle'. No one here needs to know we're related."

Parking the Land Rover in the hotel's garage, Jeremy held the door for Ellie as the pair walked in. They were immediately met by Security, a bunch of large men who looked like they meant business. But she was treated with kindness because Jeremy was their boss. He walked Ellie to her office on the third floor, helping her get settled in. Then he said goodbye and left to find his own office.

The first thing Ellie did was call her Aunt Kaitlin.

In barely a blink of an eye, Jeremy dropped by to tell her it was time to go.

"Seems like I just got here. Are we doing anything tonight?"

"Before we head to the complex, we'll visit Kensington Park and get a great view of the palace." They had a late cup of tea before taking a stroll all the way over to Hyde Park. It was almost dark when they returned to the Land Rover. Jeremy drove them to the complex.

He used a badge to access the gate to the facility. It was a series of four small buildings and one larger house. He explained that the security and maintenance staff sent over from the States by GDC occupied the smaller facilities. But they would be staying in the larger house. Because of the number of employees supporting the opening though, they would have to share the Big House—as everyone referred to it—with one other GDC employee.

Ellie knew who was staying in the big house with them and the arrangement didn't sit any better than her fish and chips.

They parked and Jeremy grabbed their luggage. She was amazed he only had one medium duffel bag, while she had three large suitcases. As they walked up the steps, the door swung open. Before her was the man she had once known, her first love. Benjamin stood framed in the doorway.

Chapter 2

enjamin smiled that crooked smile Ellie had once loved so very much. He was older, but still looked the same. He watched her face intently even as he addressed Jeremy, "Hello, boss. Good to see you. Hello, Ellie. Been quite a while, hasn't it?"

She didn't answer. She felt eyes on her. Jeremy's. He could probably see she was perplexed. Jeremy shoved a piece of luggage in Benjamin's hands and said, "Good to see you, too, Ben. Make yourself useful. Carry that up to Eleanor's room."

Ellie still didn't say anything as she stared after Benjamin. His clothes couldn't hide the muscular build. He turned and gave her a confused look before he shrugged and ascended the stairs, carrying her luggage.

For years, she'd wondered what she would say if she ever met him again. She'd played their meeting over and over in her mind so many ways. Some were romantic. Some were funny. Other times, she put him in his place—wherever that was. But now that he was in front of her, she was confused. Not only did she not know what to say, she didn't know what to feel. The look he gave her before taking her bags from Jeremy and heading up the stairs unnerved her.

As soon as he was out of earshot, Jeremy asked, "You okay? You look shaken."

He was right. The sight of seeing Ben again after all these years made her legs shaky, but she didn't know why. Was it because they'd been lovers? Was it because she was sad they had drifted apart? *Do I still love him?* She just didn't know what to say, do or feel. She took a deep breath. "I'm okay, Jeremy. It's just, well, it's been a long time since I've seen Benjamin. He looks good, doesn't he?"

Jeremy shot her a smile. "I guess so. Not too good at judging how men look. Guess I'm just not as into guys as much as you are."

His humor brought out a little laugh. "Glad you're not. If you were gay, you wouldn't be with Aunt Katie, would you?"

He smiled a sad little smile. She knew he missed his wife, who was almost five thousand miles away. His laughter startled her. "Somehow, Ellie, I believe when I saw her face, I'd have been instantly converted. When we were first together, she misheard something I said and thought I was into guys. We were just beginning to become close and I could see her fear. I laughed, telling Katie I only wanted her."

Ellie laughed with him. *You always have a way of making me feel good, no matter what.* Not for the first or last time, she was just a little envious of what her aunt and uncle had. She felt warmth in her heart. "You two are so lucky to have found each other. Tell me, what's it like to have found your true love? What does that feel like?"

He seemed to sense her insecurity. "Ellie, it's wonderful. Life's been hard on you, losing Ben and then Steve. I'm pretty sure the advice I have to give you will seem hollow, but here it comes. Katie and I both believe everything happens for a reason. God has a master plan.

I know you're young and can't wait for your life to start. It'll happen, give it time."

Her eyes were suddenly scratchy. He'd hit the nail on the head. Seeing Ben again reminded her how lonely her life was. She wanted to be loved and to be in love. That was the problem.

Jeremy pulled a couple of tissues from a nearby box and handed them to her. "Would it be better if I asked Ben to move somewhere else in the complex?"

She shook her head. "Wouldn't be fair. You can't do that to him."

He gave her a lighthearted scowl. "I most certainly can. Not only am I his boss, but I'm the Corporate Security Director. I can do pretty much whatever I please. And if I need backup, I'm pretty tight with the Director of Operations in this company." He looked around, acting like he was going to give her top secret information. "Don't tell anyone, but I sleep with her, you know?"

Ellie laughed.

His scowl changed. "We both care, that's all. If this is too much, tell me. You need to feel comfortable with the situation. How can I help you?"

She shook her head. "I just have to learn to not wear my feelings on my sleeve, that's all. I guess I need to be more mature."

Jeremy tussled her hair and teased her. "Aw shucks! My little girl's growing up! I'm so proud of you."

That brought a smile to her lips again. She hugged him tightly. "Thank you for being here with me. You two planned it this way so I wouldn't be alone. I bet you really don't need to be here. You could have done what you need to do from Chicago. But you're here. You don't know how much that means to me. Or maybe you do. Thank you! I love you, Jeremy."

"I love you too, Ellie."

As they embraced, the sound of someone clearing his throat made both of them look up. It was Benjamin. He was staring at them strangely. "None of my business, but if the two of you need me to leave... It's a little strange, since you're related, but if you're having a fling, I'll just look the other way."

Ben looked hurt. His eyes were awfully shiny. *What's that about?*

Jeremy's face turned bright red as he let go of Ellie and turned to face Ben. "It's not what you think. Nothing's going on. She's my niece, for Heaven's sake! You're the only team member who even knows we're related. I'd appreciate if you didn't mention that to anyone."

Ben's face showed anger. "Don't worry about me! I'm like Sergeant Schultz from *Hogan's Heroes*. I know *nothing!* Your dirty little secrets are safe with me. Might want to draw the blinds so no one sees anything. See you in the morning." He turned and ran up the stairs.

Ellie was flabbergasted. "You don't honestly believe he suspects us of, you know, like being together, do you?"

Jeremy's face was even darker now. "We both know nothing's going on, but after what he just walked in on? Probably suspects something. And here's another thing. I know that seeing him bothered you a little, but seeing you again bothered him a whole lot more."

Ellie's heart was racing. From seeing Ben?

Jeremy cleared his throat. "How about supper? I'm starved!"

She nodded. They walked to the kitchen, acclimating themselves to the house. The pantry was pretty bare but they found tomato soup and made tuna fish sandwiches.

After dinner, Ellie said goodnight before heading upstairs.

***

Jeremy washed the dishes, and pondered how he should approach the situation. As much as he turned it over in his head, he couldn't decide on the best solution. There was only one thing to do. He'd ask Kaitlin. She'd know. Kaitlin was the smartest woman he'd ever met. He decided to wait and call her at three-thirty A.M., after mentally converting to Chicago time which was a more reasonable nine-thirty for her. He wanted to call now, but it would interfere with dinner, bath and bedtime rituals. Katie always knew what to do. He turned out the lights, and headed to his room.

Chapter 3

*J*eremy's internal clock woke him at three-thirty. He immediately called Kaitlin's cell phone.

She answered on the first ring. "Jeremy. So good to hear your voice. I miss you so much. Do you know how hard it is to sleep without your arms around me?"

"Miss you, too. I love you, Katie. How're the kids?" They talked about little things for about twenty minutes before Jeremy changed the subject. "I think we have a problem." He told her everything about the previous night. He made sure to tell her about Ben walking in when he was holding Ellie. He needed to get that out in the open. Since they'd met, Katie's greatest fear was that he'd leave her for another woman. The sudden appearance of his ex-wife just before they got married almost cost Jeremy Katie's hand in marriage. It had almost cost him his life. "I'm being honest and wanted to let you know. There's nothing going on here."

She laughed. "We've been married for ten years. I trust you. Now with that being said, we have to be concerned about Ellie. Despite overcoming her demons, she's still vulnerable. I know we talked about what would happen when she saw Benjamin again. It didn't go as well as we had hoped, did it?"

"No, it didn't. What should I do? Should I have Ben move out of the Big House? I'm not so concerned about her while I'm here, but when I head to Edinburgh next week, she might freak out."

Katie was silent for a few minutes. "Ellie has to grow up sometime. Let's let things ride out this week. Her actions could just be jitters from seeing an old love again and nothing more than that. That's my advice. What do you think?"

He gnawed it over in his mind. "I agree. I knew you'd know what to do. I admire you for your brains, not just that sexy, perfect, hot body! You see, I married up! Jeez, you're the smartest girl I ever did meet." He paused for effect before continuing with an increasingly redneck twang. "And y'all is the gosh darned purtiest girl I ever did saw! You got them eyes that make me all goo-goo in my boots every time y'all looks my way! And that smile just makes me go all weak in my knees."

Before she could answer, a blood curdling scream echoed from down the hall, followed by the words, "No, no, no! Stop! Please stop! Help! Help!"

Kaitlin heard the words on her end. "Go! Call me back when you find out what's going on. Be careful! I love you."

Jeremy was already in motion. "Love you, too, Katie. Talk to you shortly!" He disconnected the phone. He flung open his door and headed to Ellie's room which was on the same floor, two doors down. He heard a noise. Someone running behind him. He hit his knees, swiveled and tripped the man running toward him.

It was Ben.

"Boss, what the...? What's going on?"

"Don't know yet, but I'm gonna find out." He stopped on the far side of the door, motioning for Ben to stop at the near side. Listening, he could hear Ellie softly crying in her room. Jeremy knocked loudly. "Ellie! You all right? Everything okay?"

She didn't answer immediately. There was a crash inside the room. Jeremy tried the door handle, but it was locked. He glanced at Ben. "Back me up, but don't stay too close. If someone's in there, we take him out, understood?"

Ben nodded.

Jeremy was ready to kick in the door when Ellie's voice answered, "I-I-I'm okay. I just knocked over the lamp."

"Open the door, Ellie! Now!"

"I'm coming. Let me grab my robe. I need a few seconds."

Jeremy had decided he would be in the room within ten seconds, one way or another. He started counting. At the count of eight, he heard the privacy chain being moved. The lock clicked and she cracked open the door.

"Let me in, Ellie."

Ellie pulled the door wide open. She reached for Jeremy as soon as he came in, clinging tightly.

Ben rushed past, checking out the entire room, including the private bath, under the bed, closets and windows. Seeing Jeremy holding Ellie tightly as she cried in his arms, he said, "Room's clear, Boss. You all right, El?"

She nodded.

Jeremy helped Ellie sit down on the edge of the bed. "What happened?"

She was sniffling. "I-I-I had a bad dream, a nightmare, I guess. There was a man holding me down, strangling me! I tried to get him to stop, but he wouldn't let me go!"

Ben was standing right next to Jeremy. "What man? Who was he, Ellie? Tell me who he was. I'll protect you."

She stared at him. "I don't know! A large man, maybe oriental."

"Someone you know?"

"No, never saw him before. I was on a beach and he, he just attacked me."

Jeremy brushed her hair from her eyes. "Just another bad dream. Everything's fine. You're safe, now."

Ben piped up. "I'm here for you. I'll never let anyone hurt you."

Ellie stared at him while her tears subsided.

Ben touched her arm. "Have you had nightmares about this before?"

She shook her head. "Don't know where it came from, but he was brutal. Told me he was going to kill me."

Ben's eyes were full of concern. "I imagine that was scary. You all right now?"

Ellie had a sad smile on her face. "Thank you both for coming to my rescue. I'm sorry. I'm okay now."

Jeremy nodded. "Good. Glad it was nothing. You okay if we go back to bed or would you like some company?"

She shook her head. "Please go back to bed. Sorry about this."

Ben stood there, eyes fixated on her face. "I wouldn't mind sitting with you for a little while. We can catch up on things if you'd like."

She stared back into his eyes.

Wistfully, Jeremy wondered.

Ellie shook her head. "I'm fine, really I am. Thank you both again. Good night."

Ben and Jeremy walked out into the hallway. They waited until they heard the privacy chain slide across the door jamb from inside. Looking at Jeremy, Ben quietly asked, "You think she's okay?"

"Yeah, but just to cure my inquisitive mind, do a perimeter check on the doors and windows."

"You got it, boss. See you in the morning." He turned, heading down the hallway.

Jeremy still stood outside Ellie's room when the voice of Roy Orbison quipping the two title words from his song 'Pretty Woman' sounded on his phone. Text message from Kaitlin.

'Everything okay? Please be careful! I love you forever! Call me when you can.'

As soon as he got back to his room, he redialed her number. It didn't even have a chance to ring. "Baby, what's going on? Ellie okay?"

"Everything's fine. Just a bad dream. She's good."

"I was worried about you. So Ellie had a bad dream? She say what it was about?"

"She was on a beach and some man came up and started to strangle her. What do you think brought that on?"

"I'm not sure. Did she know the man?"

"No. Maybe something she saw on TV."

"She does like to watch horror movies."

"You always say everything happens for a reason. What caused her nightmare?" Kaitlin had a minor in psychology and was pretty sharp in figuring out human behavior.

"Maybe it's being in a foreign place. London isn't Chicago, Orlando, Savannah or Cleveland. She's familiar with those cities because she's lived there. I know she's still hurting over the loss of Steve and McClellan. Loved that child like her own. She's not close with her parents or her siblings. She only has you and me. And in a couple of days, you're heading to Scotland. She'll be alone. I think that caused the nightmare."

"Should I put off going to Scotland?"

"No. She's got to grow up. Might sound cruel, but by us always being there and taking care of everything for her, she'll never regain the independence she once had."

"I feel bad, but I know she'll be fine."

"Yeah? Why?"

"Excellent stock. She's got your blood running in her veins."

"If you only knew..."

Chapter 4

The tempting aroma of eggs frying in butter drew Ellie downstairs. No new nightmares, she felt calmer now.

When she walked into the room, Ben shot her an easygoing smile. "G'morning. Doing okay?"

She felt lightheaded, seeing him. "Yes, thank you. Sorry about last night."

"It's alright. I have bad dreams sometimes when I travel, especially on red-eye flights like you had. As a welcome to England, I made your favorite breakfast. Scrambled eggs with sautéed onions, just like you like."

He'd remembered. Her heart started to flutter. She was looking for something to say when Jeremy walked in.

"Something smells good. Scrambled eggs? Cool."

Ben scooped the food onto plates, taking a tray of toast from the oven. "I know it's your first full day at the Optimum. I'll be in town all week, so if you need anything, just ask. My office is one floor down from yours." Ben glanced at Jeremy, who was keeping a keen eye on him.

"Mighty nice. Just don't forget we have a meeting from nine until noon. Maybe we'll call out for lunch."

Ben cleared his throat. "Actually, I wanted to take both of you to this little place I found. Like to try it?"

Ellie glanced at Jeremy. He smiled and winked at her. "Uh, sure. Thanks for breakfast."

***

Ellie entered the lobby when the elevator doors opened. Both men were waiting for her. Ben's smile was warm. "Morning go well?"

"Yes. Starting to get organized. Kaitlin helped me post the jobs on the internet this morning. So how close is this place? Looks like it's raining."

"Passing shower. Supposed to clear out tonight. The eatery's one tube stop down, at Edgeware."

It was chilly. Ellie hugged her arms as they entered the very crowded Bistro. As soon as Ben walked in, a short, beautiful blonde ran up to him, giving him a quick hug and peck on the lips.

Ben turned to them. "Meet Sophie. She's a travel agent for World Wind Travel and works out of one of the swanky hotels nearby."

Ellie could feel jealousy take a foothold inside, noticing how pretty she was. Short, maybe five foot one, with shoulder length hair, flawless complexion. Her build was perfectly proportioned. Even Jeremy's eyes were wide open, taking in her beauty.

Sophie ignored Jeremy and extended her hand to Ellie. "Pleased to meet you. I'm Italian, originally from a small town in Tuscany, but I've lived in London for five years. I'm Ben's girl."

His girl? Ellie recovered and took Sophie's hand. "I'm Ellie, Ellie Lucia. Pleased to meet you."

Sophie's smile split her face. "Ellie? Such a beautiful name. I'm so glad to finally meet you. Benjamin told me so much about you." Ellie glanced at Ben, whose face was turning red. "I hope you like London. Perhaps the two of us could do some sightseeing and shopping together. Would you like that?"

A calmness settled over her. Ellie gave her a genuine smile. "I'd love that. Jeremy took me on a little walk through one of the parks yesterday. London is so beautiful and I love the gardens here."

"Yes, they're quite beautiful. What do you say the two of us have dinner tonight?" Sophie winked at her. "As a travel agent, I can get us on many tours for free. Actually, there's a Thames cruise tonight that I know isn't full. After dinner, we could do that if you'd like."

So kind, but I don't want to find my way home all alone. She looked hopefully at Jeremy, hoping he would say he would go along.

But before he could respond, Sophie added, "And don't worry about getting back to the complex. I don't know if Benjamin told you or not, but I occasionally spend a night or two there. I'm sure he wouldn't mind if I stayed the night. Would you, Benjy?"

Jeremy almost choked on his drink. "Benjy? Did you just call him... Benjy?"

Her smile was enchanting. "Didn't he tell you? He's my Benjy and I'm his Sophia." The rest of the meal was spent poking fun at Ben. His face turned bright red when Sophie gushed about how much of a romantic her Benjy was.

Ellie took it all in. When it was time to go, Sophie shook Jeremy's hand, gave Ben a quick kiss on the lips and gave Ellie a long, tight hug. "Pick you up at the Optimum at five-thirty."

Ellie was deep in thought on the way back to the hotel. Ben had a girlfriend. Why didn't that bother her? Maybe it wasn't Ben she wanted after all, but the closeness they'd had.

***

Ellie's phone pinged. Jeremy had texted to tell her he'd left and wished her a fun time. It had been so long since she'd had a close friend, but meeting Sophie at lunch made her feel good. For the first time in a long time. The past two years, Jeremy and Kaitlin had been her only real friends.

The swish of the elevator door caught her attention. Sophie greeted her with a smile. "I hope you rested up this afternoon. We're going to have a blast tonight."

A blast? "What do you mean?"

"There's this quaint little place called the Red Lion Inn. They make the best Shepherd's Pie. Then, I've got two passes for a Thames sightseeing cruise."

"This is really nice. Thank you."

Sophie linked her arm through Ellie's. Her perfume was subtle, the fragrance of daffodils. "That's what girlfriends do."

After dinner, Sophie drove them down to the public parking garage near the Tower of London. The beauty of the Tower Bridge to her left, the Tower of London behind her and the London Eye off in the distance to her right were breathtaking. Sophie provided a running commentary. After the paying guests were on, they boarded the sightseeing boat.

"We're lucky. Clear nights in London are rare. Look at those stars." Sophie was a great hostess, pointing out the sights along the river. When they docked, they had to wait until everyone else disembarked. They had just reached the concrete when a tall young man approached them.

"Sophie," he cried in an accent that wasn't quite British. "You look absolutely lovely tonight." He gave Sophie a quick kiss on each cheek before turning to Ellie. He stopped, staring at her. He opened his mouth as if to speak, but no words came out.

Sophie laughed at him. "Henry Campbell! Where are your manners? I hope your Mum taught you better than to just gawk at pretty girls."

Henry blushed. He took Ellie's hand and gently kissed her fingertips. "I beg your pardon, miss. I surely didn't mean to be rude. It's not every day one of Heaven's angels comes down to earth."

The warmth flooding her cheeks made her lightheaded. She opened her mouth, but now she was the one who was speechless. *When was the last time any man complimented me like this? LIKE NEVER!* Suddenly, time stopped and the entire world faded away until it was just the two of them. She closely studied him. His light brown hair was flecked with quite a few red strands. His skin was pale, decorated with freckles. But his eyes, his eyes were green and intense.

His gaze roved from her lips to her hair. *What do you see?* As if in response, a warm smile slowly spread across his face. The warmth gravitated from her cheeks to her chest. Ellie swallowed hard, fighting back the sudden desire to taste his lips.

The peal of Sophie's laughter broke the spell. "Eleanor Lucia, may I introduce you to Henry Campbell? Henry Campbell, you naughty boy, the girl you just ogled is none other than Miss Eleanor Lucia from Chicago, America."

Henry bowed. Ellie curtsied in return. She searched her mind for something appropriate to say. Henry started to speak when suddenly, a bus horn blew three times.

Henry smacked his forehead. "Bloody hell! I forgot about my tour group! I've go to got, I mean, I've got to go!"

Don't leave, please. Ellie could only stare at him with a smile on her lips, but Sophie was laughing. "Go, Henry! Fly like the wind!"

Henry started to run off, but stopped and ran back. He grabbed both of Ellie's hands and again bowed. "Ellie, I must leave, but before I do I have to say this. It was so enchanting to meet you! I pray our paths shall cross again! Until we speak again, ta-ta!"

The bus driver repeatedly blew the horn. He turned to his bus and yelled, "I'm coming, you bloody bugger!" But Henry stopped at the door of the bus, turning toward the girls again. He waved, clenched his fist and held it to his heart for a few seconds. He entered the bus, which immediately pulled away.

Sophie laughed. "So you've met my colleague, Henry. What say we head back to the complex?" Ellie was quiet on the drive back, but her mind was relentless, remembering every detail about the man who entered the tour bus last.

Chapter 5

The delectable scent of bacon greeted Ellie as soon as she exited the shower. She hurriedly dressed and descended the stairs, heading for the kitchen. The front door opened. Jeremy, returning from his morning run, was wet not just from sweat, but also the drizzle of the morning fog. He quickly slipped his shirt on before turning toward his niece.

"Morning. What time did you get in last night?"

She couldn't contain the smile as she remembered the gentleman she'd met. "It was pushing eleven-thirty."

He kicked off his sneakers and they walked to the kitchen. "What'd you do?"

Ellie told him about dinner at the pub and the boat ride on the Thames. She held back the part about Henry Campbell. Jeremy raised his eyebrows. Did he suspect more?

Ben and Sophie were on the other side of the island in the middle of the kitchen, chatting, sipping coffee and peering into the fog. Ben suddenly turned toward them. "Hey, boss! Want some joe? What about you, Ellie? Coffee?"

Both nodded. Ellie asked the obvious. "Is that bacon I smell?"

Sophie's laughter split the air. "What is it with you Americans? Every time you smell bacon, you go crazy. I mean, I made eggs Florentine, too, but you didn't even notice that."

Jeremy stood over the pan and breathed deeply. "You just don't understand the relationship Americans have with pork bellies. I can describe it in three sentences. We love bacon, we love bacon and we love bacon!"

Sophie giggled. She didn't have any makeup on, but didn't need it. Her skin was fair, her face flawless.

Why can't I look that pretty without makeup? Ellie was self-conscious about her complexion. When she was younger, she'd suffered from a severe case of acne. She covered it every morning with heavy foundation. She turtled deeper into her housecoat, hoping no one would notice the scars.

Jeremy seemed to be entranced by Sophie. Ellie tucked that in her memory bank for later. While they ate eggs and bacon, Sophie described lovely Tuscany, where she'd been raised.

The breakfast was enjoyable. Jeremy began to clear the table. "Thanks for cooking. Ellie and I will wash the dishes."

Sophie turned to Ben, "Well, love, think I'll head off to the shower. But first, may I have dessert?" She was wearing Ben's oversized Flyers tee-shirt. She placed her arms around his neck, standing on tiptoes to kiss him. As she did, her bare buttocks were partially revealed. A rose tattoo on her right butt cheek contrasted with her creamy white skin.

Jeremy quickly turned to the sink, but not before Ellie noticed him blushing. Ellie turned as well after taking a second look. Now she really was envious. *It's not fair. Pretty and hot, too. My behind doesn't look anything like that.* Later, she'd ask Sophie about her exercise regime.

Ben walked into the laundry room. As Jeremy washed the dishes, Ellie decided to pick on him. "Like the rose tattoo?"

His blush deepened as he concentrated on the dishes. "What tattoo?"

"Yeah, right. Can't convince me you didn't see it. I saw you checking Sophie out."

His face became dark red. "Think it's gonna rain today?"

Ellie giggled. "Not allowing you to change the subject. But don't worry, you old pervert. Katie doesn't have to find out about it. Wait! What am I saying? I could use this to my advantage."

He was intently scrubbing the frying pan. "What do you mean?"

"It just might cost you. Know what I mean?"

He gave her an evil look. "What exactly is this going to cost me?"

"I don't know yet, but I'll think of something good."

"Right. Just remember, no girl's as pretty to me as Katie."

Ellie watched him. "Come on! Aunt Katie's rather plain compared to her. Sophie's a knockout. And if you're honest, you'll admit she's prettier than your wife."

Jeremy shook his head. "Sophie's attractive, but Katie's the most beautiful woman in the world to me." A devious look covered his face. "You know Ellie, me thinks you have a girl crush on your new friend. I might just have to use that to my advantage!"

Ellie's laughter bubbled over. "You know me better than that. How'd you say it yesterday... I'm not just as into girls as you are?"

They both laughed. "If you say so, Ellie."

"Okay. Let's call a truce. I won't tell your wife about your dirty little fantasies if you don't tell her about my girl crush."

Jeremy pulled the stopper and drained the sink. "Katie knows every one of my fantasies, dirty and clean. And I know every one of hers. You see, we hold nothing back between us. For when you truly love someone, you share everything."

When you love someone... and are loved by someone. Ellie was quiet as she finished drying the dishes. She headed upstairs for a shower. *Will anyone ever love me like that?*

Chapter 6

The rest of the week passed by quickly for Jeremy. He rarely saw Ellie because she and Sophie went off to sightsee or shop every evening. He was glad they'd hit it off so well. Made it easier for Ellie, but apparently not for Ben. He seemed sad, probably because Sophie was always hanging out with Ellie.

On Saturday afternoon, Jeremy was packing for Scotland when Ben walked into the living room.

Ben didn't acknowledge Jeremy, but instead walked to the window. Jeremy knew Ben well enough to know something was bothering him.

"Seems you found quite a girl in Sophie. Both pretty and kind, especially to Ellie. I'll confess, I was concerned how Ellie would react when she saw you again."

Ben turned to face Jeremy. His response wasn't what Jeremy expected. "I was worried, too. Not from her end, but mine. I was really into Ellie, you know? So stupid to let her go after college. So busy trying to make a career, I allowed our love to slip away. Did I ever screw up."

He again turned to the window with his back to Jeremy. "I flew to Orlando to beg her to take me back, but she was with some older guy, pushing a little boy in a stroller. It was too late. I left before she even knew I'd been there." Ben sniffed.

"Didn't know that. I'm sorry."

"What happened with the other guy? She looked so happy, so in love. Did he dump her?"

"That was Steve and yes, he did. Ellie followed him to Cleveland when his job moved there. We all assumed they'd get married. Then one day, he left without any warning. Reunited with his ex-wife. Life was hard on Ellie, for a very long time. We finally moved her in with us."

"Heard that. Boss, may I ask a stupid personal question?"

"Of course."

"The day you came, you two were embracing. Overheard you both say you loved each other. Are you and Ellie having a, uh, I mean, are you two in a relationship?"

Wondered how long that would take. "Relationship, yes. Fling, no. I think of Ellie as an older daughter. Sorry you misinterpreted that conversation. I'm happily married to Kaitlin. She's my entire life. I'd kill myself before putting that in jeopardy."

Ben turned to face Jeremy. His eyes were red. "Then why are you here? Everything you're doing here could have been done from the Tower. What gives?"

Jeremy sat down and sighed. "Sometimes you do things to help and support people you love. Scratch that... people you care for. Ellie's fragile. She's only our niece, but Katie and I both love and treat her like a daughter. I'm here for her."

Ben opened his mouth to say something else, but the front door suddenly flew open. Ellie and Sophie spilled in, followed by a couple Jeremy hadn't met before.

The smile on Ellie's face was like summer sunshine. "Jeremy, hi! Brought a couple of friends over for dinner. This is Henry Campbell and his girlfriend, Heidi Fries."

Jeremy extended his hand to Henry. The glint in Henry's eye and straight-as-a-knife-blade stature said it all. "Pleased to meet you." Jeremy turned to Heidi. She was plump, profusely tattooed and her closely cropped hair was bright purple. "Pleased to meet you, ma'am."

Heidi giggled. She returned the pleasantry before turning to the other girls while Jeremy turned his attention to Henry. "Forgive me for asking, but the way you carry yourself, would you be active or former military?"

Henry grinned. "Could ask you the same thing, sir. Served Her Majesty in the Royal Marines, six years. The last two were spent in the Special Boat Service. Could tell at a glance you're former military. Which branch were you in?"

Jeremy's chest swelled. *It was an honor to serve.* "U.S. Army, fourteen years, all of that in the Rangers."

Henry's eyes opened wide. He again shook Jeremy's hand. "So honored to meet you. Rangers did quite a lot of work in the Middle East. Were you in Iraq or Afghanistan?"

"Multiple tours, both theaters. Special Boat Service, you say?" Henry nodded. "Were you also deployed in the Middle East?"

Henry laughed. "I could tell you, sir... but I'd have to kill you."

***

Ben felt left out as Jeremy and Henry swapped service stories. He hadn't served in the Armed Forces, the only one of Jeremy's direct reports who hadn't. Ben always felt self-conscious around former military types. Many of them, but strangely not Jeremy, seemed to look down on him, although they never said anything to his face.

Despite a house full of people, Ben was lonely. Ellie hadn't said hi when she returned. Neither had Sophie. So after he poured another cup of coffee, he headed to the kitchen. Staring out the window, he noted the rain seemed to be letting up.

The touch of a hand on his shoulder interrupted his thoughts. It was Jeremy. "What do you say we take the girls out to dinner? You pick the place."

Ben's spirit lifted. It was nice to be included again. One thing Jeremy did well was read his feelings. "I think that's a great idea." He called to the girls. "Ladies, how about dinner? Anyone have suggestions on what cuisine for tonight?"

Sophie walked in and gave him a peck on the lips before she traced his jawbone with her finger. "If you don't mind, love, I'd like to stay in and make dinner tonight. I was planning on fettucine and broasted lamb."

Her eyes asked the question as much as her words. So beautiful. *How could I refuse?* Ben nodded and Sophie rewarded him with a wet kiss. She turned to the group. "I'm in the mood for pasta and roasted lamb. How does that sound?"

Everyone readily agreed.

Sophie grabbed his hand. "Come with me, love." She led him outside. Her warm hands were a contrast to the chilly air. She kissed him again. "The reason I want to stay here is because I invited another boy to come over tonight."

Ben felt his eyes involuntarily open wide. "Another boy?"

She laughed. "Benjy, not for me. You remember William?"

The guy who creeped him out. "The weird front desk guy from your hotel?"

"Yeah, and he's not weird. I invited him over tonight. To introduce him to Ellie."

Introduce him *to Ellie?* "Why would you do that?"

"I want her to have someone, too. Look, I miss being with you. I'm spending all my time with her. And every minute I spend with her is a minute I don't spend with you."

An eerie feeling climbed his spine. "No one asked you to spend all that time with her. You don't need to do that. It's nice, really nice, but unnecessary."

Her smile left her face as she searched his eyes. He suddenly felt naked. "No, I do need to do that."

"Why?"

She kissed his hand and sighed. "Oh Benjy, you're a bright boy. If I didn't keep her occupied, she'd have spent all week home, with you."

Ben's cheeks heated. He searched his mind for something to say, but she put her finger to his lips. "Don't even pretend you don't have feelings for her. I see it in your eyes. Maybe I'm greedy, but I'm not going to take a chance on losing you to some American girl. She had her time. It's my turn now!" Her lips found his and remained there for a long time. She slid his hands around her waist. "I hope you know how much I love you, Benjy."

Chapter 7

*J*eremy packed his last few items as Ellie and Heidi gave Sophie a hand in the kitchen. The food smelled luscious. They were just about to sit down to eat when the doorbell rang. Jeremy stood to answer it, but Sophie yelled, "I've got it."

Henry and Ben were seated across from him and Jeremy noted both sets of eyes grow dark. He turned to see what they were staring at. An average height man with short, dark brown hair stood at Sophie's side. He carried an air of superiority and stroked his impeccably trimmed mustache.

"Everyone, this is William Canterbee," Sophie introduced. "He works at the hotel with Henry and me. I invited him to dinner." All hands said hello. Sophie led him directly to Ellie. "And William, this is Ellie Lucia from Chicago, in the States. Ellie, this is William." He gracefully bowed to her. "William, you can sit next to Ellie. I laid out a plate for you."

William held Ellie's chair for her. As the meal progressed, Jeremy watched all three younger men. Sophie had apparently just set up his niece with this gentleman. Jeremy's observation revealed William was overly formal, quite proper in his mannerisms. But something about him bothered Jeremy, though he couldn't immediately identify what it was. Jeremy came to the conclusion he didn't like William, at all. As he glanced around the table, he found he wasn't the only one watching William. Both Ben and Henry were glaring at him like a pair of hawks. *What's that about?* They appeared anxious, like a spring ready to release, if Ellie needed them. It dawned on him. Both of them were jealous.

After dinner, Jeremy excused himself so he could Skype with Kaitlin and their children.

***

Ben rolled his eyes when the girls decided to play a game of Scrabble in teams. It was interesting, using a combination of British, American and Italian words. Ellie was smart. She and William quickly pulled out to an early lead. Ellie seemed to thrive on the attention William gave her.

Ben sat across the table, quietly fuming. *Why am I so attracted to Ellie?* It wasn't her appearance. In no way whatsoever could she compare to Sophie's beauty or perfect build. No, that wasn't the attraction. His mind drifted back to when they'd been a couple. He realized he missed their closeness. They'd been at the point in their relationship where they seemed to be able to read each other's minds, finish each other's sentences. Ellie made every day a celebration. She'd surprise him with picnics between classes. Leave him little gifts.

William made some stuffy remark, which Ellie responded to with a laugh.

Her daily love letters had been so sweet. Ben closed his eyes and remembered the scent of the perfume she sprayed on the envelopes. Ellie had made his life something special. His mind drifted back to a spring weekend long ago. The college had been deserted for the holidays. He went to her dorm room and found a post-it note on the door. *Find me and you can have anything you want...* The cross-campus scavenger hunt led him to twenty different locations. In each, he found her suggestive notes. Four hours later, he finally found his prize on the fourth floor of the library, reading Romeo and Juliet. Ellie gave him everything he dreamed of that night. As he looked back, he realized he'd held his every desire in the palm of his hand. And he'd thrown it all away.

Sophie topped off his glass of wine, giving him a quick peck on the lips. He wished those lips belonged to Ellie. *Idiot! Why'd you ever let her go?* He'd loved her, but he didn't realize how much until he'd let her slip away.

Dammit, he'd allowed his feelings to show. Sophie had noticed. If he wasn't careful, he'd end up hurting her, too.

Do you ever miss me, Ellie? Still love me? What would he do if she did? Would he leave Sophie for her? He really didn't know, but watching her bond with William was killing him.

***

Henry sat on the other side of the table, jealously watching William work his charms on Ellie. He had disliked William since the first time they'd met. He didn't know him well, but if William did half the things he'd heard, he was a horrible man.

Heidi excused herself to freshen up. Probably needed to apply more gel to keep her close cropped, purple hair standing on edge.

Henry's thoughts drifted back to Ellie. She'd been on the forefront of his mind since they'd met. He was entranced. She was all he'd thought about. Last week was his turn to work the evening shift, so he hadn't had the chance to come up with an excuse to see her. He'd thought about getting someone to take his tours, but Sophie was the only other possibility on such short notice.

Henry glanced across the table at his friend. She was smiling as she watched William and Ellie with apparent keen interest. Sophie was his closest friend, but he dared not tell her how he felt about Ellie. Sophie's lips were looser than a worn out bearing. Another reason not to tell Sophie was because Heidi was her best friend. All week long, he'd had to bite his tongue as Sophie went on and on about Ellie. But a nagging thought pestered him. Something about the way Sophie had bonded so quickly with Ellie wasn't right, yet he couldn't understand what it was.

Heidi returned, breaking his concentration. Henry noticed Ben and William standing. He realized Ellie was excusing herself from the table. Henry quickly stood until Ellie had left the room.

Heidi punched his arm. "Why don't you stand when I leave the room?"

Maybe if you were a lady like Ellie. "Sorry, love. Just following their actions."

Everyone was silent until Ellie returned. Again, the men stood. Heidi pinched the back of his leg while he was standing. He ignored her.

The game went on. Henry made sure Heidi didn't see him looking, but he gazed at Ellie quite often. She was very pretty, but there were two things that attracted him to her immensely. Those dark brown eyes of hers almost drove him out of his mind. They were so large and her eye shadow accentuated them. He'd heard an American story once, about the beautiful 'doe eyed' girls. The story was true; her eyes melted his heart.

Almost as if she read his mind, Ellie turned, looked in his eyes and shot him that treasure of a smile. It lasted only a few seconds before she turned her attention back to William. Henry had to force himself to breathe. Those dimples! When she smiled, she had two dimples. One on her right cheek and a second on her chin. Her dimples were his second favorite thing in the entire world. He suddenly added a third and a fourth thing to 'Ellie's List'—her lips and her voice. If he could only hear one sound ever again, he'd want it to be her voice. As he sat there next to his girlfriend of three months, he couldn't help but wonder what Ellie's lips tasted like.

The night ended too soon for Henry. They said goodnight to everyone before he drove Heidi home. The silence in the car was deafening.

Heidi interrupted his train of thought. "You're quiet, Hen. Something on your mind?"

He forced a yawn. "No, just a bit tired, that's all."

"What do you think of our new American friend?"

He knew Heidi well enough to see it was an expedition to uncover his innermost thoughts. Henry acted as if he had to think about who Heidi was talking about. "American friend?"

"Ellie, the girl you gawked at all evening."

"Oh her? She's nice, I guess. What do you think of her?"

She laughed and turned away. "Okay, I guess. Sophie doesn't trust her, though. You pick up on that?"

He *had* been right. Time to dig into Heidi's girl radar. He made sure to reply with apparent indifference. "I didn't quite get that. Why'd you say that?"

Heidi yawned. "Sophie told me so."

What? "I thought Sophie and Eleanor were the closest of friends!"

Heidi grunted a laugh. "Ever hear the saying, 'keep your friends close, but your enemies closer?' Seems our American friend and Benjy were lovers, for about three years."

Henry almost swerved off the road. *Ellie and Ben?* What had she ever seen in him? And Ben? He must have been insane to let Ellie go. *If she were mine, I'd move mountains to keep her.*

Heidi's voice caught his attention. "And with her staying in the same house as Ben, Sophie's worried. She thinks Ben still has a thing for the little tart. Since Sophie has evening tours this week, she's concerned the hussy will make her move. That's why she invited William. She gave him specific instructions to keep Ellie occupied and out of Ben's sight."

Henry was glad it was dark so she couldn't see his face as he drove her home. "She gave William instructions? Why would he do what she says?"

Heidi's laugh was maniacal. "Hen, are you that simple? Sophie and William have had this on again, off again love affair for years. Even though she's dating Ben, she still beds William every chance she gets."

Henry was having trouble keeping the car on the road! "Really? What's she see in William? Is she in love with him?"

Heidi laughed so hard Henry was afraid she would fall off the seat. "Hell no! It has nothing to do with love!"

This didn't make sense. Sophie was the purest girl he'd ever met... well, maybe until Ellie. "If Sophie doesn't love him, why would she sleep with him?"

Heidi's voice was soft. "Don't you know? William's a gigolo. When he turns on the charm, no girl can resist him. Do you know how many girls he's slept with? Hundreds. Sophie's hoping if he gives it to Ellie, she'll forget about Ben."

The braised lamb was threatening to make a re-appearance. *Never thought Sophie would act this way.* He thought he knew Sophie better than that. Something dark and nasty crawled up his spine and planted itself in his brain. Henry quickly identified it. Fear, for Ellie. He didn't know her well, or really at all. But the thought of William seducing Ellie... His mouth was suddenly dry. His heart raced as he drove along.

Heidi's voice again broke his trance. "I know what you're thinking, Hen. And the answer's yes."

What? He shot a glance at her. The question he was really pondering didn't have a yes or no answer. "Yes to what?"

Slight hesitation. "Yes, to the question of whether I slept with William. He and I had a fling a couple of months ago. Before I met you."

This conversation was becoming way too much for Henry to handle. William had seduced Sophie, then Heidi? And Sophie was trying to get him to do the same thing to Ellie? He struggled to keep from vomiting.

"You slept with him? Why?"

"Sophie told me she'd slept with him. Other girls did, too. I wanted to see if he was the tiger in bed everyone said he was."

He lifted his head and swallowed the vile tasting phlegm. "Was he?"

Her laugh this time saddened him. "Oh yeah! Best shag ever."

Henry was quiet. *I don't know you, at all.* He could feel Heidi's eyes boring into him in the dark.

"Now don't act all high and mighty on me. Come on, spill the beans. I know you shagged girls before. Don't try and tell me you never did a girl just because she was pretty or built like a goddess."

Henry hadn't. Any interest he'd ever had in Heidi was fading rapidly. "Actually, Heidi, both girls I slept with were long term girlfriends, very long term. And we were in love. Did you care for him at all or was it just for the sex?"

"Care for him? Hell no! You've got to be kidding. He's not my type." Heidi's voice was much softer. "But you are. My type, I mean." She ran her fingers through his short hair, but Henry pulled his head away. "Bet you're wondering, if I'm that kind of girl, why haven't you and I slept together? Am I right?"

Henry was relieved they hadn't slept together. Only within the last week had they started kissing. This conversation was contributing to his upset stomach. "You don't have to explain."

"I want to. He didn't mean anything to me, just a fun roll in the hay. But you? I'm seriously interested in you. I don't want you to think I do that all the time. That's why you and I haven't done it. But tonight's your lucky night. Come up to my flat with me. I'll take care of what ails you."

Henry pulled up to her building and stopped along the curb. He didn't shift to neutral or even apply the parking brake. He focused his eyes on a distant traffic light.

Heidi exhaled sharply. "Well, I can see my honesty wasn't something you wanted tonight. Sorry about that, love. Will you be stopping by tomorrow?"

Henry's nausea wasn't just because Heidi had told him about her fling with William. It surprised him that he was more concerned about Ellie and the plot Sophie had unleashed. "I don't know about tomorrow. I've got a few things to do. Let me think about it."

A car went by and he felt her eyes study his face in the headlights. "All right, I see. We'll play it by ear. Just as a reminder, I'll be in Dublin Monday through Thursday. Can we plan on dinner next Friday?"

This was his out. He needed time to think about everything. "That would be lovely. Pick you up at six Friday night." He gave her a quick peck on the cheek before driving away.

Chapter 8

*O*ophie had breakfast waiting when Ellie descended the stairs. So she *had* spent the night with Ben after Jeremy left for Scotland. After the meal, the three headed into the city. Ben pulled the car to the curb at Sophie's hotel. She was in the front while Ellie was seated in the back.

Sophie leaned over to give Ben a long kiss. Her whisper was loud enough for Ellie to hear. "I have to work late tonight, but I'll call you when I get off. I love you so much."

She directed her attention to Ellie. "Sorry, I'll be working late, but you'll get a surprise this evening."

Ellie climbed out of the back seat to sit up front with Ben. She was excited. "A surprise? What is it?"

"Now, if I told you, it wouldn't be a surprise, would it?" They shared a quick hug before Ben pulled away. Sophie looked so sad.

Travelling toward work, Ellie noted the faraway look in Ben's eye. *He misses Sophie already.* Love was a wonderful thing. *Wish the love bug would bite me.* "I'm really happy for you. Sophie's a wonderful girl."

"She's okay," he responded quietly.

What? "Just okay? The way she talked, I thought you two were head over heels in love. Don't you love Sophie?"

43

He shot her a look she didn't recognize. So much irritation in his voice. "Does it really matter to you?"

His tone annoyed her. "You two have a fight or something? If so, don't take it out on me."

The car swerved on the road. "No, we didn't have a fight. I simply asked you a question. Does it really matter to you?"

"Does what matter to me?"

He pulled the car over, took it out of gear, and set the brake. He turned to face her. "If I'm happy. Do you care at all?"

She shrugged. "Of course. I want you to be happy."

"Does it bother you that I'm with her?"

Where was he going with this? "Her? You mean Sophie? Why should it, Ben?"

His face reddened. "Do you ever have regrets we broke up?"

She shuddered as she thought of the past. "I don't want to go there. Let sleeping dogs lie."

"Okay, then let me answer. I screwed up, El. I regret leaving you."

"Ben, don't do this..."

"Did you know that after you moved to Orlando, I came to see you? Letting you go was the biggest mistake I ever made. I came to beg you to take me back, but you were pushing some kid around in a stroller, drooling over that guy. Looked so happy. I left."

Memories of the past roared into her thoughts. Not all were good ones. "Don't do this. You belong to Sophie now. Let it be."

"I can't. I thought I could, until you showed up here. Then, when I saw your face again..."

Isn't this a hell of a way to start the week? "Stop it right now, Benjamin. You're making me uncomfortable. One more word and I'll walk the rest of the way to work."

"Ellie, all I want to know is..."

Screw this! Ellie threw the door open. "This is *not* happening. Drive yourself."

She was about to close the car door when he snarled, "Get your ass back in the car. I'll take you in."

She didn't even bother giving him the courtesy of a return comment or gesture. She walked across the street and headed down the sidewalk to the hotel.

***

Sunday dragged on unmercifully for Henry. With nothing to do in his little flat, he took a drive in the country. Heidi called him a bit after eight, but he didn't want to talk to her, actually ever again. *We're through.* Her confession about her fling with William bothered him, but not nearly as much as Sophie's plan to deal with Ellie.

He was upset with Sophie. She'd been his first friend when he came to London. While there was no romantic connection between them, they'd always been close. When he couldn't go home to Scotland at Christmas, he and Sophie had spent the holidays together. They talked, ran around and shared everything, or so he thought.

He stopped at the top of a hill to take in the view. Hearing about Sophie and William had shocked him. The thing that made him mad was that Sophie asked William to make a move on Ellie. *I hate that man.*

He wracked his brain all day trying to come up with a way to prevent William from seeing Ellie. Late in the day, a plan came to him. He could protect Ellie, if a little bit of luck fell his way.

Monday morning, he arrived at work to help load the bus for a multi-country tour group. They pulled away from the curb a little before eight. As Henry straightened up to ease his aching back, he saw Ben's car pull up to the curb. He watched Sophie climb out. When Ellie climbed out and hugged Sophie goodbye, Henry bit his tongue.

Sophie's betrayal was on par with what Judas Iscariot did to Jesus. He walked in to wash his hands, gathering his thoughts before confronting his friend.

***

Sophie sat down. The room smelled musty. *Benjy!* Since Ellie appeared, their closeness had diminished. The slamming door startled her. It was Henry. "You scared me. Don't do that again. You'll give me a heart attack!"

His voice sounded like he was mocking her. "Oh, I'd never want to do anything like that to you, Sophia. I mean, you should always be treated in the kindest, gentlest way possible."

He'd used her formal name. She raised an eyebrow. "Are you okay?"

"I was."

"You was, I mean, were? Something happen? What's wrong, love?"

"I'm feeling a little sad... and hurt this morning."

"What happened? You can tell me."

"It's so nice to have someone care. You see, I learned something very shocking about someone I care about, or rather, did care about very much. I'm saddened to think she's that kind of girl. Never gave me a hint she was like that."

"It's Heidi, isn't it?" Sophie put her own problems away. Henry needed her. She didn't think their relationship stood much of a chance. Heidi was too much of a party girl. She'd never settle down with just one guy. Poor Henry, so innocent and sweet. "I should have warned you about her. Never wanted you to get hurt."

His laughter was like thunder. "Warn me about Heidi? Not want me to get hurt? It's so kind of you to care so much for others." He was sarcastic. "It's not about

Heidi. You don't have a blinking clue what I'm talking about, do you?"

Something was terribly wrong. "Did I say or do something wrong?"

"Bloody hell right you did!" he screamed. Frightened by his outburst, she backed away. "You don't have a flipping clue why, do you? Damn you, Sophie, damn you!"

This was too much. Her breath came rapidly and her vision blurred. Having Henry angry at her was more than she could handle right now. Her response was weak. "I'm not feeling the sharpest right now. Whatever I did to offend you, I'm sorry. I need you, especially now. Enlighten me, please."

He plopped into the chair, wiping his eyes. His words were measured. "It's not one thing, it's two. They're related and right now, I don't know which is worst. Is it because you weren't honest with me or because I never once in a million years believed you had a cruel bone in your body?"

If he'd been anyone else, Sophie would have told him to bugger off. But like it or not, she needed Henry. He was her anchor. "You're right. I don't understand. Guess I'm stupid. Tell me what I did."

He closed his eyes and took a deep breath. "First, I really don't know you. Thought you were the sweetest girl in the world, pure and extraordinary. But after what Heidi told me, you're a common slut."

Her world was crumbling. First Benjy, now Henry. "What? What did she say?"

"She told me about your fling with William..."

You have no right. That's my personal life. "I don't have to tell you everything. Don't think..."

His face was red and the veins on his temples were bulging. "Let me finish. She assured me when you aren't sleeping with Benjy, you're doing it with William. After the way you went on and on about how much you loved Benjy, how could you? If that isn't being a slut, I don't know what is."

Her vision tinged red. Fists curled, her face almost touched his. "If you have to stick your nose in my business, let me set the record straight. Your girlfriend lied."

He was still mocking her. "What? She lied about you sleeping with him? That's what she alleged."

"Don't doubt she did. I'll set the record straight. Her hair color isn't the only thing that's wild. Did Heidi tell you she belongs to a club to pick up men and couples?"

Henry took a step backwards. "N-n-no."

"I'm not like Heidi." She drew a deep breath. "Remember when I broke up with that engineer from Delhi?"

Henry's expression was less severe. "You were so in love."

Sophie swallowed hard. "That's right."

"When he left, you were distraught."

"He got what he wanted, then dumped me. He was the first man ever, Henry. But he didn't love me, he used me. I was vulnerable. William flirted with me and for God knows what reason, I let him take me home. That was the only time."

His expression changed. Henry felt her pain. "I never slept with William again. I was simply a conquest. Think what you want. I'm not the kind of girl who does it with any bloke that looks my way. None of your business, but I've only slept with three men."

He reached to touch her. She drew away from him. "Some things I'm not proud of. But what hurts worse than remembering my mistakes is being judged by someone I love, by my best friend. By you."

Henry recoiled. "Someone you love? Me? Your best friend? Heidi's your best friend."

"Please. You should know how I feel. I have few friends, boy or girlfriends. Women fear I'll take their man away. Men want to get me into bed. Heidi wanted to be my friend so she could pick up the men I turned down."

Sophie brushed her cheeks with the back of her hand. "But you? You were the only person I could be myself with. I could tell you anything and everything without worrying about it being blabbed to everyone. I never worried about being judged, until now. I should hate you, but despite your shortcomings, I still need you."

Henry studied the floor. "I apologize for judging you. But there's one thing I can't understand. Since Ellie came here, you two have become dear friends. If you felt bad for sleeping with William, why would you do this?"

Her chest tightened. *I wish you could understand.* Her voice was barely a whisper. "I'm scared."

"Scared of what?"

"I'm scared to death of, of... her."

Henry's mouth dropped open. "Ellie? Why?"

"She and Benjy were lovers. I'm afraid she'll take him from me. Ben's the one person I want to spend the rest of my life with. I love him, but for whatever reason, she has a hold on his heart." She fought back a sob. "The first time he and I made love, he called me Ellie." Her shoulders heaved as her sorrow grew. "In his mind, she's perfect! I can't compete with that. When he told me that she was coming to England and staying in the same house he was, I almost gave up hope. I thought about leaving him, but Henry, I can't. I need him like I need air to breathe. Can you understand?"

He grasped her hands. "I'm sorry, Sophie, but you've got to stop this thing between Ellie and William. He'll only use her. That's not right. Call him off."

Sophie softly touched his face. "You fell for her, too. I see it in your eyes. You love her. Ellie's something very special and me, I'm nothing."

Henry hugged her tightly for a few seconds. "You're special to me, but this isn't right." He pushed her to an arm's length. "In your heart, you know this is wrong."

She softly kissed his forehead, drawing him into a hug. "I'm too scared of losing Benjy. If it comes down to Ellie or me, she's going to lose every time I hope William does whatever he needs to do to keep her away from Benjy. If that's wrong, I apologize. Maybe someday you'll find someone you love so much that you'd do anything to keep. I hope you'll forgive me. If you can't, my life will be forever saddened."

Sophie dried her eyes before heading out to the restroom. The rest of the morning, they didn't say another word to each other.

Chapter 9

Ellie had just finished a phone interview when Security informed her Henry Campbell was waiting in the lobby. She was curious. *Why would he be here?* When the elevator doors opened, Henry stood to greet her. He looked so cute.

"Henry! This is a surprise." His hair was damp from the rain. "What can I do for you?"

He started to blush. "Actually, it isn't what you can do for me, but what I can do for you."

Her palms were suddenly sweaty. "What you can do for me?" She bit her lip as she waited for his reply. Henry seemed to be searching for something to say, like a school boy who'd forgotten his lines. When she started to giggle, his face turned bright red. "What is it, Henry? Don't keep me in suspense!"

He cleared his throat. "Since Sophie's busy this week, may I take you sightseeing?"

Is this a dream? "I'd be honored. Where are we going?"

His mouth dropped open and his eyes grew wide. It was obvious he wasn't prepared. "Uhh, tonight's a surprise."

A wonderfully warm feeling started in her chest and spread down her limbs. "I love surprises!"

"Great. I've, uh, got to get back. Meet you here at six?"

"Sure."

He bowed and held his closed hand to his chest. "I'll see you then. Good day."

She curtsied. "Until we meet again." His eyes grew large and his face turned even redder just before he departed.

Her mind was spinning. An explainable tingling filled her chest. Ellie texted Ben she wouldn't need a ride that evening.

Within seconds, a reply appeared on her phone.

'Who's taking you home? William?'

Then her phone rang. Also Ben. She ignored that call as well as his next ten. She finally silenced her phone.

The afternoon seemed to drag on for weeks. A conference call with the home office ran much longer than expected. She hoped Henry would still be waiting. As soon as the elevator doors opened, Henry jumped to his feet. *He's so adorable.* The rest of the world faded away. Ellie breathed evenly to prevent herself from running to him.

Henry reached for her hands. "You look spectacular! How was your day?"

So warm, so natural. She felt playful. "Fine, except for one thing."

His eyebrows raised. "What's that?"

"I couldn't concentrate."

He looked worried. "Something happen?"

Ellie failed miserably in her quest not to smile. "Actually it did." She covered her mouth.

"Don't keep me in suspense."

She pinched herself to keep her laughter at bay. "Well... This nice Scottish gentleman stopped by earlier.

He told me he was going to take me away somewhere as a surprise, but he kept *me* in suspense." She held her chin between her thumb and forefinger as she stared into space. "I wonder where he'll whisk me off to..."

His relief was evident. "Shall I tell you now or just keep you wondering?"

She squeezed his hands tightly. "Tell me now. I can't wait! I've been looking forward to this all afternoon. Please, please, please tell me."

He winked. "Sophie said you like the Royals. Is that right?"

"Yes, yes."

"Great. Thought we might visit Kensington Palace and stroll through the gardens. I hope I'm not being too forward, but I brought a picnic supper for us to share. Perhaps at the Lady Diana memorial. Afterwards, I'll take you to see Buckingham Palace just as the sun sets. Would that be all right?"

The room was suddenly warm. She could barely contain her excitement. It was like he knew her already. "I'd love that."

***

Henry felt like a prince. Ellie took his arm as he escorted her to his car and opened the door for her. They parked near the palace entrance.

They walked past a tea house. "Jeremy took me there my first day," she said. "It was wonderful."

The way she said Jeremy's name puzzled him a little. "Is Jeremy your colleague?"

Ellie stopped and turned, her smile fading. The look concerned him. "I don't know you well," she said, "but I want to ask you something. May I?"

Damn. Jeremy was more than a colleague. He tried to hide his disappointment. "Of course. Ask me anything you desire."

She leaned in closer. Her perfume filled his lungs. Henry closed his eyes. Fresh apricots.

"Can you keep a secret?"

"A secret? Of course."

She paused, briefly searching his eyes, "You can't tell anyone. Jeremy's my uncle."

His face must have shown his relief. Ellie laughed. "Did you think I was going to say something else?"

He felt his cheeks heat. "Actually, I was afraid you were."

"Like what?"

He looked away. "I don't know, like maybe you were in love with him or something."

As she smiled, her dimples came out. "I do love him, but not romantically. He's like a father to me. I can't wait to introduce you to Kaitlin, his wife. They're very special to me."

After seeing Kensington palace, Henry led her to the Diana memorial. The fountain was deserted. Henry laid out their picnic meal. Ellie slipped out of her shoes, dipping her feet in the running water. As they ate, they talked about their lives.

"I grew up in Savannah, Georgia. In the American south. I'm the oldest of six kids. How about you?"

Henry opened a container of fruit which they shared. "I was raised on a tiny sheep farm in the Scottish lowlands, a wee bit from Glasgow. I've two brothers and a little sister. Great place to grow up."

Ellie recalled her college years. How she and Benjy had been lovers, but he left her after graduation.

Her hand trailed in the running water. "I fell in love with a kind man named Steve. He had a son whom I adored. I thought Steve was the one, that we'd get married. Then one day, he left. Went back to his ex-wife." Ellie's eyes were moist. "I started drinking to ease the pain. I was in a downward spiral. Kaitlin and Jeremy saved me. She hired me and helped me rebuild my life. That brought me here to you, uh, I mean London." Ellie blushed and looked away. "What about you?"

Ellie's openness surprised him. *She trusts me.* Henry smiled inside as her brown eyes watched him. "Always thought I'd be a farmer. Fell in love with the girl next door. When she died, I couldn't stay there. Every blade of grass reminded me of Annie."

When Henry stopped to wipe his cheeks, Ellie took his hand and squeezed it tightly. "I'm sorry, Henry."

He nodded. "I joined the Royal Marines to get away. The last two years were spent in the SBS, Special Boat Services. A lot like American Special Forces. When my enlistment was up, I found myself here, working with Sophie as a travel agent." He had to fight the urge to sweep Ellie into his arms.

After dinner, while Henry tidied up, Ellie kept her feet in the water. She seemed to be lost in thought. She jumped when he broke the silence.

"May I dry your feet?" Her eyes glistened as he gently dried them. *Such gorgeous eyes.* Her feet were beautiful. He felt her studying him. When he was finished, he glanced at her face. *She's blushing. Why?* His heart was pounding uncontrollably. Her feet had been warm and soft, just like her hands.

Ellie touched his face. "Thank you for tonight. It's been wonderful."

"We're not through. I've one other place to take you. Will you walk with me?" Without a word, she linked her arm and they walked into Hyde Park. The scent of apricots filled his being. It was as if the entire world vanished, except for where she touched him.

The sun was setting when they arrived. The reflections of the sunset brilliantly lit up the windows of Buckingham Palace. Ellie removed her arm from his, then slowly intertwined their fingers. *This must be Heaven.*

Ellie's head rested on his shoulder. "You're so lucky to live here. Like a fairy tale."

The sight was spectacular, but the real beauty was the girl holding his hand. He had trouble breathing. *I'm the luckiest man alive.* In his entire life, he'd never felt what was running rampant inside of him. Henry fought off the urge to kiss her brow. Instead, he simply rested his head against hers.

In a soft voice, Ellie whispered, "Thank you so much for this magical evening. So special."

"No. Thank you. May I ask you something?"

She squeezed his hand tightly and turned to face him. "In a moment. I need to tell you something first."

Henry knew what he wanted her to say. Feelings were building inside him. A few more seconds and he wouldn't be able to control them. "Yes?"

She searched his face. Yet again, the world rolled out of focus. Nothing in the universe mattered, except Ellie.

She started to giggle, but covered her mouth. She managed to get out the next sentence with a straight face. "You give a much, much better sightseeing tour than Sophie." They both laughed. "Now, what do you want to ask me?"

"May we continue sightseeing tomorrow night?"

Ellie sighed. "Thought you'd never ask."

Those beautiful eyes... Once again, her dimples appeared.

Chapter 10

The musty smell was so irritating, Sophie sprayed her perfume in the office. Henry had given her the silent treatment all day long. *Such a horrid day*. Nothing went right. First, she had a very nasty customer who insulted not only her nationality, but her intelligence. Then, one of the female hotel staff happily pointed out she had a run in her stocking. Finally, Henry left for the evening without so much as a goodbye. *I'm so lonely*. She didn't have many friends. Her family was non-existent.

She called Heidi to hear a friendly voice, but her friend was beside herself. "Henry won't answer my calls. He's going to dump me." It was obvious the girl had been drinking. Sophie took the first opportunity she could to hang up.

Her loneliness prevailed when she returned to her little flat. The bitter taste of hot tea was no help. She missed Benjy. *I need to hear his voice*. He didn't answer the first ten times she called. On the eleventh time, his angry voice greeted her. "What do you want, Sophie?"

Her spirits dropped. She stammered her response, "I-I-I just missed you, love. Am I bothering you?"

"Where's Ellie?"

What? She'd only wanted to hear his voice, but he asked about *her*? "How would I know?"

"Spill the beans. You did something to keep her away. Where is she?"

Sophie's world was disintegrating before her. She needed Ben's love and understanding, but his thoughts were obviously on Ellie. Anger sprouted within her. "Why do you care so much about that girl? I thought you loved me."

"Never said I didn't," he shouted. But his silence spoke volumes. He hadn't said he loved her.

She had trouble getting the words out. "If you do, why is she the first thing you ask about?" More silence followed. Tears blurred her vision. "You still love her, don't you?"

It was a while before Ben answered. His voice was softer. "I never meant to hurt you. I just need to find out where this thing with Ellie is going to go."

Thing with Ellie? "What are you saying?"

"Sophie, just send her home. I don't know where she is, but you do."

She was having trouble getting the words out. This was intolerable. "I haven't the foggiest."

"I don't believe you."

"Please, Benjy, I'm telling you the truth."

"Whatever!" He disconnected the call. Sophie stared at her phone in disbelief. Her heart threatened to beat out of her chest. She needed Henry, so she texted, asking him to call her. She waited five minutes, but there was no reply. Again, she texted:

'It's an emergency!'

No response. She waited ten minutes before calling him. No answer. She kept calling until a man's voice answered Henry's phone.

"Hello?"

"I'm sorry," she responded, "I was trying to reach Henry Campbell." She glanced at the display. It was Henry's number. "Wait! Who are you and why are you answering his phone?"

"I'm a police officer, ma'am. Who are you?"

A policeman? Fear gripped her heart. She'd die if something bad happened to Henry. She struggled to control her voice. "I'm his friend. Is he all right?"

"I've no idea. I'm at the Diana memorial. Was walking past when I heard a mobile ring. Who does this phone belong to?"

"Henry." Sophie couldn't help it. A sob escaped her throat. "Henry Thomas Campbell."

"I see. How shall I get it to him?" Sophie told him where they worked. "I'll swing by and drop it off at the desk," the policeman offered.

Alone in her room, Sophie cried herself to sleep. There was no one to comfort her in the worst day of her life.

***

Ben was worried sick about Ellie. He hadn't been in the office when she texted. Her lack of response to his texts unnerved him. He wanted to talk with her. He'd spent the last two days thinking about his feelings. Ben realized he was in love with her, now more than ever. She had to feel the same way.

At seven, there was a knock at the door. Ben yanked it open to find William standing there on the stoop holding a bouquet of flowers.

"Good evening. Is Eleanor in?"

Ben was seething. It rubbed him raw the way Ellie and William had bonded during the game night. So William was interested in Ellie? *Not on my watch.* "She's not here. What do you want?"

"I wanted to drop by to see her. I've flowers for her."

"She's not here."

"When do you expect her?"

"How the hell should I know?"

Ben's rudeness didn't seem to bother William at all. The picture of self-confidence. "I see. Mind if I wait inside for her?"

"Yeah, I do."

"Well then. Would you kindly hold these flowers for her?"

"Sure." Ben ripped the flowers from William's hand and slammed the door in the idiot's face. Ben threw the flowers in the kitchen garbage can on the way to grab another beer. His anger grew as he waited for Ellie's return. His anger multiplied as the hours passed. The girl had a lot of explaining to do when she came home. And she would answer to him. In more ways than one.

***

Ellie noted it was pushing eleven when the headlights reached the complex. Henry opened her car door and offered his arm. They strolled, very slowly. *He doesn't want the night to end, either.* Under the glow of the porch lamp, they stared into each other's eyes. Every other sight vanished. Time stood still. Henry's eyes searched hers, occasionally dropping to her lips. Not a word was spoken. Tonight had been perfect. *Kiss me.* But as she studied him, she felt he was struggling with something. She began to understand. He didn't kiss her because Heidi was his girlfriend. There'd be no goodnight kiss. The trance was broken.

Ellie ended the silence. "Tonight has been wonderful." *No, magical.* "Thank you so much. Still want to get together tomorrow?"

He trembled. "Yes, yes, I certainly do. May I pick you up at your work tomorrow night?"

She smiled sadly and nodded. Then she couldn't help herself. She grabbed him, pulling him in to a very long and tight hug. She had to hug him so he wouldn't see the moistness... or the longing... in her eyes. "It's so wonderful over here. I don't have many friends."

Ellie released him to look at his green eyes. "First Sophie and then... you. Both such good friends to me." She wasn't sure because of the dim illumination, but she could swear she saw anger in his eyes. *Why?* Her body became stiff as she stared in bewilderment.

When he noted the question in her eyes, his demeanor softened. "That's because finding a girl as enchanting as you is like finding a needle in a haystack ten miles high. You're a very special girl, Ellie Lucia. I hope you realize that."

His expression touched her. "Thank you, Henry. Finding friends as wonderful as you—I mean the two of you—has been such a godsend. You don't know what this evening has meant to me."

It took them another fifteen minutes to finally say goodnight. Ellie was having such a hard time not pressing her lips to his. She wanted to discover his taste, explore his world. Instead they shared another very long hug before he bid her goodnight one final time.

Her chin quivered as he walked away. After he opened the car door, Henry started frantically searching his pockets, then inside the car for something. What was he looking for? He finally climbed in, waving and holding his fist to his chest. Ellie returned the wave, slowly clenching her own fist to her heart. As his headlights faded, sadness enveloped her.

Gazing at the sky, clouds were beginning to cover the moon. Tomorrow would be another rainy day. Her thoughts drifted back to the man in the car. She really, really liked Henry, but he was with Heidi. Ellie didn't like to judge people, but she wondered what he possibly could see in that other girl. Before she slipped her key in the lock, she hugged herself, wishing she was hugging Henry again.

As soon as the door closed, lights flooded the room. Ben stood with his arms crossed and a wildness in his eyes. "Where the hell have you been?" he roared. "I've been worried sick about you."

His attitude was irritating. Ellie stood her ground. "None of your business, Benjamin."

"Who were you with?" he demanded.

She started to walk toward the kitchen. "Again, none of your business."

He grabbed her arm and violently swung her around to face him. "Damn you, woman. I love you. I'm making it my business." He grabbed the back of her neck and roughly pressed his lips to hers. The smell of beer on his breath sickened her. She struggled, but his grip was too tight. "I love you so much, El. I missed us. I'm going to make love to you tonight, baby, all night long." His free hand sought for, and found her dress zipper. He pulled it down. It took all of her resolve not to fight back, but he was too strong. Ellie bided her time. Ben gently massaged her shoulder before dropping below her waist. "All night long. Over and over. Just like the old days."

Ellie was going to defend herself, but needed more space. Instead she kissed him gently. "Let me do it. It's a new dress."

Ben relaxed his grip and dropped his arms. Her hand was on his shoulder. She grabbed a handful of hair and drew her right arm back to gain swinging room. With everything she had, she drilled her fist right into his solar plexus.

Ben instinctively surged forward, but she intensified her grip, keeping him upright. She pulled her arm back again and struck him squarely in the nose with the base of her hand.

Blood spurted out and he heaved forward. She slammed the pointed heel of her right shoe down onto the top of his bare left foot.

Ben howled in pain. Ellie shoved him backwards, delivering a devastating kick to his groin. Ben toppled to the floor and rolled to his side.

Ellie stood over him. "Just to make it perfectly clear, I do *not* love you. Try that again, Benjamin, and I'll press charges. Got it?"

He moaned and rolled away from her. She kicked his ribs hard and screamed, "Answer me! Did you understand what I said?"

Through his pain, he groaned. "Yes, yes, I understand."

"Remember that." *Asshole.*

Ellie walked into the kitchen and grabbed a bottle of water from the fridge. That's when she saw the flowers in the trash can. She retrieved them, reading the note. "Dearest Ellie, know that in my eyes, these flowers could never be as beautiful as you are to me. Please call me. William." His number was written on the card. As she climbed the stairs, she thought about both William and Henry. Henry was the one who set her heart on fire, but he was with Heidi.

After sliding the privacy chain across her door, she decided to wait and call William in the morning. She had liked him when he came over on Saturday. Well, a little. Maybe she'd give him a try. But despite logic, it was Henry who held her hand while they strolled through the forest of her dreams.

Chapter 11

*H*enry arrived early to search for his phone. *Where is that damned thing?* A front desk clerk walked in. The flirty one who was always snippy to Sophie. The one he didn't like. She was exceptionally chipper. "Morning, Henry. The police dropped off your mobile. Found it in the park. Thought you might like to have it back. Do I get a reward?" She pursed her lips.

He thanked her and turned away. He decided to call Heidi. But before he could unlock the screen, it rang. He didn't recognize the number. "Hello?"

As soon as he heard the voice, he smiled. "Morning, love."

It's Ellie! She called me 'love'!

Ellie laughed at his silence. "Cat got your tongue this morning, Henry?"

His face crinkled into a smile. "It's so good to hear your voice. How on earth did you get my number?"

Her laughter made his heart flutter. "Last week Sophie used my phone when her battery gave out. I saved your number. I'm a sneak, aren't I?"

He was as giddy as a schoolboy. "Not at all. You seem to be in a particularly good mood today. Any special reason?"

"Umm. Maybe. I want to ask a favor."

A favor? The pitch of her voice had changed. *Why?*

"Anything, for you."

She hesitated. "I'm out of practice. Bear with me."

Henry's curiosity turned to concern. "I don't understand. What's going on?"

"Henry, I, uh, I wanted to ask if you would..." She grew silent for a second. "I wanted to ask if you'd have lunch with me today."

Henry almost fell off the chair. "Name a place and a time and not even the Queen's army could keep me away."

She sighed, audibly. *Relief?* "I was worried you'd turn me down."

Never. "Why would you think that?"

Silence. Concern reared its head. "Are you still there?"

He heard her take a deep breath. "Yes, sorry. I get distracted sometimes, like, oh look! A squirrel!"

He didn't get the joke. "Squirrels? Why did you think I'd turn you down?"

More hesitation in her voice. "I don't know. Like maybe... maybe you're tired of me."

"Are you kidding? You're the most interesting girl I've ever met. I'll never grow tired of you, not in a million years."

She giggled. "Thank you, Henry. I have to catch my ride into work. Can we meet at the Bistro near Edgeware station, say around eleven-thirty?"

"Splendid! I'd be delighted." He needed to let her know. "Ellie?"

"Yes?"

"Thank you. I shouldn't tell this, but I want you to know... you're very important... to me. Bye-bye."

***

Ellie hung up. Inside, her heart was doing somersaults. There *was* something there. The chemistry she'd felt was real.

Ellie turned. Benjamin was behind her, staring at her. He had two black eyes. From last night when he...

He nodded. "Morning, Ellie."

She showed no emotion. "Benjamin. Will you drive me in or should I find another ride?"

"I'll take you in, but I need to say something."

She shook her head. "Don't start this again."

He held up his hands. "Wait, just listen. This isn't a come-on. I was drunk last night. I owe you an apology. What I did was wrong. I'm sorry."

He shifted his weight and looked away. "I can't change the way I feel, but I can and will change my actions. Forgive me. Give me another chance. I'd like to start over again."

"Ben, I'm not interested in you. Please..."

"I get it. I just don't want anything weird between us. I only want to be friends. It was just when you came back, I thought everything I'd lost had returned. Everything I wanted in my life was finally here."

Ellie was already walking toward the door. "Let's talk as we ride to work, okay? I have an interview first thing this morning and can't be late. But I'm curious, what exactly do you want?" Ellie turned to face him. "Don't you dare say it's me or I'll call a taxi."

He locked the door behind them and turned to her. "I want exactly what we had, Ellie. I want love. I want closeness. I want someone to share my life with."

She was perplexed. "You already have it."

He looked at her with hopefulness. "I do?"

"Yes, you do. Sophie is hopelessly in love with you. When she and I were together, you were all she talked about. True love is rare, but it's in the palm of your hand."

She thought she could read his mind. "As far as you and me, don't think I don't feel a spark. I still care about you. You knew how much I loved you, but what's past is past. Forever. We'll never be a couple again. Get it out of your mind. Even if I did want you, I'll never take another woman's man, especially not from a friend as close as Sophie." *Or Heidi?*

She shook the thoughts away. Ellie studied the bushes along the fence. How could Ben be this stupid?

"If what you're telling me is really what you want, open your eyes. Sophie loves you. So much it hurts her. Be the smart and caring man I remember. Don't throw away what you have because of something you wish you hadn't given up."

Ben wiped his eyes. "I guess you're right. Didn't consider how she felt. We were dating, actually we were doing a lot more than dating. Didn't see it until now."

Idiot. "You should. The way she looks at you is exactly how Aunt Katie looks at Uncle Jeremy. They have true love. Sophie loves you much more than I ever did, hopelessly in love with you. Everyone can see it. Can't you?"

He didn't meet her gaze. "Guess I'm stupid."

"Wise up quickly. Girls like her, beautiful inside and out, are rare. I guarantee if you lose her, you'll regret it for the rest of your life. Now let's get going." The drive into London was in total silence.

Ellie's thoughts were on Henry. His eyes, his smile, and the way they shared when they talked. Her mind drifted back to last night. It was as if no one else existed. The night had been... almost perfect. Like they'd known each other since birth. She felt so close to him. Was that why she'd bared her soul? Everything had changed, in just a few hours.

Rain started sprinkling on the windshield. The time they'd spent together was a tiny fraction of her life, yet so significant. She couldn't believe she'd asked him to lunch. And their date last night? She sniffed. Not really a date, just time together between friends, close friends.

A double decker bus cut them off. Did she mean what she'd said to Ben? About not taking another woman's man? Even if that man was Henry Campbell? If he and Heidi were serious, she'd have to distance herself. If she could. But if they weren't serious? *Probably ponder that all morning.* But her heart quickly answered the question.

***

Henry's morning was so busy, he didn't get a chance to look at his phone. He'd hoped he could call Heidi, but didn't have the chance. He hadn't even had time to look at his texts. Sophie walked in as Henry was putting on his mac before heading to the Bistro. One quick look revealed something was very wrong. Sophie's makeup was smeared.

He reached for her, but she maintained her distance. "What's wrong?"

"Get your phone back?"

"Yes, how'd you know it was missing?"

"I tried to call you last night. I needed you. I'm desperately in need of a friend."

He checked his watch. "As much as I want to, I can't right now. I have an engagement."

"Henry, I feel like I might die if I can't talk. Please?"

Henry noticed her eyes. Bloodshot and red. His heart went out to her, but he was already late. He hugged her. She clung tightly to him and sobbed.

"Back in an hour, I promise. Can you hold out that long?"

"Do I have a choice?"

He kissed her cheek before leaving.

As soon as he crossed the threshold, he felt Ellie. She was there, somewhere. Henry scanned the crowd until he saw her, sitting at a small table in the back. Even from a distance, her twin dimples were evident. *Ellie.* She waved at him. He smiled and worked his way to her. She was standing, arms open. *Like coming home.* He held her tightly, absorbing her scent. Why was her essence so irresistible?

"Hi. I was afraid you wouldn't see me stuck here in the back."

He had to force himself not to kiss her. "You look spectacular." He smiled. "Actually, I felt you before I saw you."

Ellie's smile grew even wider. "You felt me?"

They sat at the table. Henry couldn't let go of her hand. "Soon as I arrived, I could tell you were here. After that, it was simple to find you." His heart was smiling, too.

Her brown eyes grew larger as she searched his. "How was it simple?"

"I looked for the most beautiful girl here." Her face blushed, bright red. He squeezed her hand ever more tightly. "I found her. It's you."

She squeezed his hand briefly in return before pulling away. She studied her placemat. "I need to say something. I haven't shared what happened in my life with many people. Until I told you, only Katie, Jeremy, my Mimi and Papaw knew everything. My parents don't know the whole story... like they'd even care."

Her eyes met his with the intensity of a tidal wave. Something more came through, her feelings. *Best thing ever.*

She grabbed his hands again. "But it felt so natural to share my story with you. When I left America, I felt so insecure. But something happened last night, like I'm cured. I feel whole inside again. Maybe later I'll regret opening up to you, but I feel like I've known you all my life. Like you were there with me... through thick and thin. What's happening?" She squeezed his hands and released them.

Henry's mouth was dry. He didn't know what to say, yet. *Could it be she really is the one?*

Ellie looked away. "I'm sorry, Henry. I shouldn't have said anything, but I'm finding it hard not to tell you what I feel inside."

Henry wanted to tell her exactly how he felt. But he was a gentleman. He needed to talk to Heidi first.

Henry coughed into his hand. "Thank you for sharing. Believe it or not, my feelings pretty much match yours. You know about my childhood, growing up lonely on a sheep farm. Except one thing. For my entire life, I knew there was someone with me, someone I couldn't see, but rather felt. Ever since I was a wee little one. I always wondered who it was."

Henry bit his lip. Time to reveal his heart. Those brown eyes melted away every barrier. "Until you showed up. Just now when I walked in, what I felt was the person who was always with me was here, right in this place, right now. It's you. Ellie, I..."

He couldn't quite finish it. Henry relaxed his head to study the ceiling. His feelings were so strong. *Am I in love with her?* Should he tell her? What would she say or do? This was so out of character. Always so careful, quite reserved, stiff upper lip and all that. But this beautiful, dark-haired, brown-eyed, American girl sitting close to him blew him away. He couldn't help but feel this way about her. If Ellie asked him to jump out of a tenth-story window, he would, without question.

Ellie lightly touched his hands. Her voice was quiet. "Yes?"

He looked intently into her eyes. It happened again. The entire world melted away until the only thing he saw was Eleanor Lucia's eyes and face. His eyes searched hers. Slowly, a wide smile covered her face. She squeezed his hands so hard it hurt.

Her laughter broke the trance. "Are you a hypnotist? Just now, I felt it too." Her smile disappeared. "I felt it, Henry, inside my soul, as surely as you are holding my hands. Like we were one." Her face rapidly paled. She shoved his hands away and looked everywhere but at him. "We have to stop this."

What? "I'm sorry, I don't understand. Why do we have to stop?"

When her eyes engaged his, they were moist. Henry swore he could feel sadness emanating from her. "You have a girlfriend, that's why."

The words tumbled out. "If I didn't, would that make a difference?"

Her mouth dropped open. "Do you?"

"Do I what?"

Hopeful. Demanding. "Do you have a girlfriend? Is Heidi your girlfriend?"

Dammit! He'd been too busy to call Heidi. "May I defer that question until our outing tonight?"

She frowned and shook her head.

Please understand. "I want to answer that question, fully, but as a gentleman, I need to do something first."

***

Ellie's tone was firm. "What do you need to do?"

"I can't tell you, just yet. But I promise I'll tell you everything. Please trust me. May I answer you fully tonight?"

Again she frowned, shaking her head no. "That's why I wanted to have lunch with you. I can't go out tonight."

His eyes widened.

She cocked her head. How strange. She could feel his emotion. Was it fear? She shook off the thought. "The reason I can't go sightseeing isn't because I don't want to, believe me. I forgot I'd promised Kaitlin, to Skype with her children tonight. Apparently they miss me."

For whatever reason, she could feel hope start to build inside of him.

"All right, how about tomorrow night?"

Her bottom lip stuck out. "Sorry. William asked me on a date tomorrow night and I accepted."

Her mind recoiled from the intensity of emotions. Not hers, Henry's. *What the...?* Devastation and fear. His eyes welled. What in the world...?

"You can't go out with him. Please don't!"

"Why?"

"Because."

Something was wrong and she was dying to know what it was. "Give me a better excuse than just 'because', please?"

Panic replaced devastation. Tendrils of fear crawled up her spine.

"I have a counter-suggestion. May I come over tonight after your call? I promise I'll explain everything."

The look on his face welcomed her fear to surface. Was it because of what she'd seen in Henry's eyes when she mentioned William? "That might work. I planned on calling them about ten. We could do dinner, at my place."

Wait. Steve used to do this. Used to amplify his emotions to sway Ellie's opinion. But Henry wasn't expressing them, not verbally. No matter, this felt like a ploy.

"No, wait a minute. Before we discuss dinner or anything else, I want your honesty. What's going on?"

"I know this sounds quite peculiar, but I'm afraid for you."

What? The feelings were total honesty. However, her fear again came alive. "You're afraid for me? I don't understand. Does it involve William?"

He was breathing hard. "Yes, it does."

None of this made sense. "What is it?"

"May I explain it tonight?"

Anger came out of nowhere. "Don't play head games with me, Henry Campbell. I need to know right now. If you're afraid for me, I need to know why and I need to know now."

He shuffled around in his seat, like a child who was caught in a lie. "Ellie, it's not what you think, not a normal date. That's all I can say right now. The rest will take a while to explain, but I really, really need for you to hear me out. Unfortunately, I don't have the time this second. I must leave. The Agency scheduled a rare afternoon tour. Believe me, if there was any way I could stay and explain it all now, I would. Please trust me on this."

"Leave? But you haven't had lunch yet. That is why you came, isn't it?"

"Actually, no. I came to see you." His hand was shaking. "I can imagine how this seems, but Ellie, you are important to me, so very important."

Ellie couldn't recognize Henry's feeling inside, but it felt good. Really, *really* good.

"And I owe you the answer to not only the question about William, but also about Heidi. This must sound strange, I know, but please trust me on this until I can explain it all tonight."

What in the world was going on? Was he a lunatic or did she really have something to worry about? *He's not crazy.* She'd feel it. Would it hurt to wait until she saw him tonight? Something was bothering him very badly, that she knew. Was it simply because he didn't want her to go out with William?

She sat up straight. "Henry, I barely know you." He winced. Pain. "But, somehow, I know that you feel whatever is bothering you is in my best interest to know, isn't it?"

"Yes."

"All right then, go back to work. Drop by around seven. I'll make fried chicken." Immense relief.

"That would be lovely, but realize something. I don't care what we eat or even if we eat together. It's not about that at all. It's because I want, no, I *need* to see you."

A terrifying thought entered her mind. "Am I in any danger?"

"No, not right now. You might even think it's nothing. Things are happening around you that I will explain. You need to know everything before you go out with him, that's all." He must have felt her puzzlement. "I know how this must seem, but Eleanor Lucia, trust me, please?"

She'd only just met Henry. Could she trust him? Overwhelmingly, her heart said 'yes'.

"I do, Henry Campbell, I do."

He stood to go, waiting for her to stand. She didn't. He took her hand, squeezing it tightly.

"Hear me out tonight. If you think I am being stupid, tell me so. If you do, I'll never bother you again. But in my heart of hearts, I really think you'll want to know what I have to say. Goodbye, my dearest friend." With that, he held his fist to his chest, turned and left. He reached for his phone before he made it to the door.

What just happened? It was so strange, the way she felt his feelings. That had never occurred before, with anyone. Had she become a psychic? It didn't matter. Joining with Henry's soul was the best thing that ever happened.

Her mind was fully on Henry... and his girlfriend. She finished her tea and dried her lips with the napkin. She whispered out loud, "Heidi Fries, you're in for the fight of your life. I'm going to win your boyfriend's heart."

Chapter 12

*S*ophie was a mess after Henry left. She needed him desperately. He was the only friend she had left, the only one she trusted. When Henry returned, the obvious anger on his face scared her. Sophie couldn't help it. She began to cry.

His hands gripped the air, as if he wanted to choke her. He finally spoke. "Damn you, Sophie. Why'd you do this?"

"What did I do?"

"You sicked William on that poor girl. Why?"

"I already told you. I'm scared of her."

"And because of your fear, you're willing to sacrifice Ellie?"

"Sacrifice her? You act like I asked William to kill her."

"Kill her, seduce her and God knows what else. Is there a difference?"

"You don't know her like I do. She took Benjy from me."

"What?"

She was having trouble seeing. "When I called him last night, he told me he had to see where this 'thing with Ellie' was going to go, then hung up. He's put our love on hold. He won't answer my calls. Can't you see she has him in her claws?"

Henry shot her a look of confusion. "We're not talking about the same girl. Ellie didn't take Benjy from you. If she did, I would've felt it."

Sophie's crying increased in intensity. "She took you from me, too. She has you wrapped around her little finger."

Henry shook his head. "You're wrong. It's all in your head. We're through, Sophie. I can't tolerate this anymore. I have a tour starting in a couple of minutes. Goodbye."

She fell to her knees and grabbed his arm. "Please stay. My world's upside down. Don't go on the tour. I need you more than ever."

Henry tried to pull away, but she clung tightly. "I'll do anything. You're the only friend I have left. Stay with me. Talk with me. Comfort me. Please?"

He studied her briefly. "Do you really want my friendship?"

Hope glimmered in her eyes. "Yes. More than anything else."

"Then call off this thing with William. Do that and we go back to the way we were, otherwise, we're through." He turned, grabbed a clipboard and jacket and left.

Her heart was breaking. Damn that Eleanor Lucia! Her only friend had chosen the other woman over her. Who did she need more, Benjy or Henry? While she wanted Benjy, she needed Henry's friendship. Without it, she'd die.

After Henry left with the tour, the office was quiet. As Sophie touched up her makeup, she made her plan. Ellie would not take Henry from her, too.

Sophie walked to the hotel desk, motioning for William. He took note of her, finishing up with his customer before approaching.

"Our plan's right on track. I'm taking the Yankee out tomorrow."

"I need to talk to you about that. Break off your date with Ellie."

He stared at her with curiosity. "Why? I like American women. They have no inhibitions."

"Please. I never should've asked you to do this."

"But you did and I'm up to the challenge." He shot her a lewd wink. "I'll take care of what ails her."

She shuddered at his inference. "Forget about her and call off your date."

He took a step back. "Why would you ask that?"

"I am asking for a friend."

"Must be a damn good friend. You begged me to get her attention."

"I know, but now I'm asking you to forget it. Please?"

His face slowly turned into a leer. "I can be persuaded, but I expect a favor in return."

"And what would that be?"

"You replace her."

Sophie's mouth dropped in horror. "What?"

He ran his tongue over his lips. "I'll back off, but I'll need a replacement. You'll do fine."

"Please no. I'm in a long-term relationship."

He shrugged his shoulders. "Doesn't matter to me. I'll do the American instead."

"Maybe she won't want you."

His laugh was evil. "Never had a girl turn me down. They might say no, but that's not what they *really* mean."

"No, please."

"Up to you. Take it or leave it. Text me either way."

Sophie almost threw up. She had no choice. Eleanor Lucia was going to win, again.

***

The enticing scent of frying chicken warmed Ellie's heart, as if she needed anything else. *Henry will soon be here.*

Ben walked into the kitchen. "That smells wonderful."

She turned, laughing before shooting him a happy smile. "Hope you're in the mood for home cooking." Her smile disappeared. "I do have a favor to ask, though."

"What's that?"

She felt her cheeks warm. "Henry's coming over. We have something important to discuss. Would you mind eating somewhere else instead of with us?"

He winced, but nodded. "I'll go into town and eat at a pub or something."

Ellie shook her head. "No. I remember how much you loved fried chicken. I made it for you."

"Okay." Ben looked at her wistfully. "I've got a few movies I haven't watched yet. I'll eat in the other room." He reached across the counter, offering his hand. Ellie squeezed it gently. "I meant what I said earlier. I can't change how I feel, but I am changing the way I act. Sorry about last night."

She patted his hand. "Me, too. Sorry about your eyes."

He shook his head. "I deserved it. Need help with supper?"

"Nope! Got it all under control."

The doorbell rang. Her heart started to flutter.

"That's Henry. Mind answering that?"

He gave a sad smile as he walked toward the door.

The text alert on Ellie's phone sounded.

'Something came up. Can't do our date tomorrow. Know you'll understand. William.'

What? Why had William cancelled?

Henry's aftershave caught her attention. He was soaked, but carried a bouquet of pink roses. *Did he know pink's my favorite color?* All thoughts of William dissipated. Henry's smile made her lightheaded.

"Evening, Ellie. Sorry, I got caught in the rain without my mac. What is that delectable aroma filling the air?"

Were the butterflies in her stomach from his comment or just because he was here?

"What beautiful flowers. Are they for me?"

Henry nodded.

"Thank you." She placed them in water and continued, "I made a meal from the American South. Fried chicken, courtesy of my mother's recipe, homemade mashed potatoes with gravy made from scratch and black eyed beans. You hungry?"

Henry's face was beaming. "Famished, but I hope you realize, it's not the food I came for."

Ellie knew she was turning red as she gave the gravy one last stir.

"May I share something while you cook?"

"Actually, it's ready. Help me fix the plates."

"What's wrong with the plates?"

She laughed. "That's American slang for putting food on them."

"I see." Henry held the plates as she dished out the food. "You asked me a few questions today that I promised I'd answer. The first was about Heidi and whether she is my girlfriend. When we were talking today at lunch, she *was*."

The inflection in his voice caught her attention. "Was?"

His green eyes twinkled. "I broke it off with her this afternoon."

Ellie put down the spoon and drew close. It happened again. The entire world only consisted of two pair of eyes closely searching the opposite pair. "Did you break up with Heidi because of me?"

The depth of his gaze seemed to go on and on. "Yes, and no."

"How can your answer be both?"

"It's easier to answer the 'no' part first."

Henry grew silent as he studied her lips.

"I'm all ears, Henry."

Suddenly he laughed, breaking the trance that held them. "Oh Ellie, there's so much more to you than your ears."

She giggled and jabbed him in his ribs. "Jerk. All this time I thought you liked me for my mind, not my body."

"I do... and other things, too. You have the most beautiful eyes, and your smile? It melts my heart. Why did you call me a jerk?"

"Forget it. I was teasing you." They were back—his feelings. *So special.* "Please continue with what you were saying."

"That relationship wasn't something I wanted anymore. When Heidi told me what Sophie had done, Heidi also told me what she did with William."

Ellie was confused. "Sophie, William, Heidi? I don't understand this at all."

Ben's voice suddenly came from behind them. "What did Sophie do?"

Ellie turned her head from him. "Sophie introduced William to me."

"Oh, okay. I'm going to eat in the other room. I'll wash the dishes as a thank you." Ben left the kitchen.

When Henry turned toward her, she placed her forefinger against his lips. Her smile was gone. "Let's wait to continue our conversation." Henry nodded. "So how was your day? Tell me all about it."

Ben wasn't paying attention, but they kept the conversation bland anyways. After carrying their empty plates to the sink, Ellie took Henry's hand. She led him to the rear door and grabbed a large umbrella.

Henry balked. "It's pouring cats and dogs out there."

She turned to him and smiled. "Do you trust me, Henry Campbell?"

"Absolutely, I do."

"Then follow me."

Henry took the umbrella and instinctively wrapped his arm around her. Ellie didn't protest and directed him to a small swing, well hidden from the house by the grape vines. She reached into a small covered box, removing two plastic seat cushions. They had to snuggle closely to stay dry.

"I'm sorry this isn't ideal. I'd rather see your face, but I don't want Ben to hear. Do you mind?"

"This might be a sticky conversation and I'd rather see your eyes, too. Is there another option?"

"Maybe, wait a second." She changed her position and knelt on the swing to face him.

"That looks uncomfortable."

She grimaced. "It's not the best."

"Let's go inside."

She shook her head. "I want privacy."

"We could go to my car and talk face to face."

Nodding, she answered. "We could, but your car is out front, in direct sight of every other house in the complex. I hate prying eyes. This is private. I want to talk here."

"Then you should sit and I'll kneel."

"One of us will still be kneeling."

"What do you suggest?"

Ellie hesitated, her heart rising in her throat. "I could sit on your lap?"

She felt his answer before he spoke. He loved the idea.

"Are you sure?"

Ellie nodded. She moved, sitting on his lap. Her face had to be close to his so they could stay under the umbrella. Henry's scent filled her being, and it sure wasn't his aftershave. It was how he smelled.

"Yes."

He studied her eyes briefly. "Are all American women as forward as you?"

She returned his gaze. "I don't know. Don't think I'm like this all the time or with everyone." She bit her lip. "I shouldn't tell you this, but you're special, Henry. There were three things I felt, no, *knew* when we met." She stopped, her eyes searching his. She could feel his trepidation.

"What were they?"

She took a deep breath. "The first thing was that I can trust you, totally. I can, can't I?" He smiled and nodded. She felt a warmth from inside him. "The second thing I knew was that you liked me, instantly. Am I right on that?" He blushed and nodded again. "The third thing was," she hesitated, now biting her lip. "The third thing was that I instantly liked you. Something very special happened in those fifteen seconds when we met. When you kissed my hand, it was a feeling I've never felt before." Her cheeks were on fire. "Did I say too much?"

He shook his head, smiling very broadly. Joy. "No. I felt the same way. I wanted to tell you the same thing, but you beat me to it."

Ellie grasped his free hand and squeezed it tightly. "Well, now we have a base to work from. Tell me about Heidi. You said the reason you broke up was both because and not because of me. Please explain."

She felt him shiver, but the warmth from him grew. He took a deep breath. Anxiousness. "On Saturday, Heidi and I had a long conversation on the way home. We'd been dating for a couple of months, but it wasn't going anywhere. She and I kissed, maybe three times, but I didn't feel anything at all. The differences between our lifestyles were too great. Then, she told me some other things I couldn't stomach. I felt we were through, but I gave it some time to really think about it. I came to the realization I didn't want her. But, as a gentleman, I needed to tell her first. After lunch, I finally got a hold of her. I told her she and I were done."

Despite wanting Henry, her heart went out to Heidi. "How'd she take it?"

"She said she knew it was coming. Told me she'd decided if I didn't break off with her, she was going to break off with me. Afterwards, she got angry, saying things I'm sure she didn't mean. I felt bad for her, but sometimes, relationships just don't work out. She has to accept that."

Ellie frowned. "I'm sorry. That's the part that didn't concern me?" He nodded sadly. "Would you like to go on or is this too difficult?"

"No, I told you I'd explain totally. The part that concerns you, you already know. My feelings matched yours. The feelings about you were so strong and warm when we met. I only hoped you'd feel the same."

Concern that she was acting like Steve's ex-wife bothered her. "I'd never steal a man from another woman." A strange feeling was coming from Henry. Ellie couldn't identify it. Something was on his mind. "What are you thinking?" She felt sadness, yet something else.

He shook his head. "You didn't steal me from her. We were through."

"But if I hadn't come along, you would still be with her."

His smile was sad. "We might have stayed together for a little while, but it was going to end. And it wasn't because of you."

Could she believe him?

As in response to her thought, he said, "As time goes on, you'll find I'm an honest man. And for some reason, I don't think I could ever hide anything from you. Do you believe me?"

Ellie searched his eyes. Did he break up with Heidi because he thought Ellie was more attractive? *No.* Warm feelings again flowed from Henry.

"It would be hard to believe those words from any other man. I'd suspect they had different plans." She felt his pain. "But I do believe you. To give me a clear conscience, I need to ask once more. Did you break up because of me?"

His eyes were clear. Honesty. "No, it wasn't because of you."

"Then, unless you have more to say about Heidi, can we close that chapter?" He smiled and nodded. Relief flooded her soul, hers and his. "Now, tell me about William and Sophie."

His face clouded as he looked away. Anger. "This will sound like a lie. I'm ashamed to tell you."

"I need to hear it."

He suddenly turned to face her. Fear now mixed with anger. "Sophie's my best friend. Never been closer to anyone. Like a sister. I love Sophie, but not in a romantic way. She's treated you like her best friend in the world, hasn't she?"

Ellie's face beamed. "Yes, she has."

His eyes narrowed. "But she's lying. The only reason she wanted to be close to you was to keep you from Benjamin."

What? "Keep me from Ben? What's that supposed to mean?"

"Sophie told me that Ben still has feelings for you. The other day he told her he was putting their relationship on ice, to see where it went with you."

Ellie vividly remembered what Ben had tried to do. "When you came in tonight, did you take a close look at his face?"

"Uh, I was more interested in seeing you."

"His two black eyes are courtesy of the heel of my hand. I made it extremely clear I wasn't interested. Is that why Sophie's mad at me?"

"No, she befriended you to set you up with William. He's a womanizer, only interested in one thing. Sophie hoped you'd fall for him. She's scared to death of you. She loves her Benjy, but knows he still wants you."

Ellie's mouth dropped open.

"That's why I'm begging you not to go out with William. You're only a conquest to him. Sophie wanted him to bed you so you'd forget about Ben. You're too special for that. Please don't see him."

Sophie? How could she? If what Henry was saying was true, she and Sophie were going to have a come to Jesus meeting. She bristled and pulled away from Henry. Rain poured down on her.

Henry shifted the umbrella to keep her dry. Her anger was so strong, she could no longer feel him. "Let me tell you something, Henry Campbell. I might have seemed forward with you, but make no mistake, I'm not that kind of girl. No one could make me do anything I don't want to do."

"I never thought that, but he has a reputation for getting what he wants, whether his partners are willing or not. Hearsay only, but I've heard it quite a few times. From more than one person."

She stared in disbelief and stood. He adjusted the umbrella again. Over her anger, she felt sadness. Horrible sadness. His.

"I can see you didn't like what I said. Promised if you thought I was a buffoon, I'd leave you alone. I'll go now. Hoped it wouldn't end this way, but even if I just made you aware of his intentions, it was worth it."

He handed her the umbrella, moved her aside and stood.

She could only stare as the rain soaked him head to toe.

Before he turned away, he muttered, "Goodbye, Ellie. It was an honor to have known you. I wish you well in all you do." Eyes down, he started to walk away.

"That's it? You said your piece and just leave? What the hell? I expected so much more from you."

"I know you're angry," he turned back, "but I don't know what else I could have done."

She fought back her anger. "Damn right, I'm upset. As far as expectations, I didn't think you'd give up on us just because I got mad. Don't you understand? I'm pissed at Sophie, not you. Why would she do that to me?"

Her breath was rapid and shallow. Ellie searched his eyes.

He dropped his chin. "I'm sorry, Ellie."

Please understand. His thoughts looked like sorrow. Deep, deep sorrow. He turned to leave.

Ellie threw down the umbrella and ran to him in the pouring rain. Her chest heaved against his ribs. "I haven't had a close friend for so long, but I thought I'd found one in her. Why would she betray me like that?" Pulling away, she searched his eyes. "Am I some miserable, horrible beast to be dealt with?"

He brushed her wet hair from her eyes. "No," he said softly. "To me, you're the most wonderful woman God ever created."

Her tears stopped as she stared at him. Suddenly, she felt his intentions. Crystal clear. *He loves me.*

"You didn't have to tell me any of this, did you?" she whispered.

He shook his head as he shivered in the deluge.

"You could have watched it unfold from the sidelines and picked up the pieces afterwards. Would've been much easier. But instead, you thought I'd send you away, forever. Believed I was angry at you. Thought we were over, for good. I felt your heartbreak inside of me, but still you told me. Why?"

He wiped her tears away. Gently. "I did it because even if you sent me away, I care about you. Immensely. I always will." His face matched his feelings. So sad.

She threw her arms around him, clinging tightly to him once again. "Henry Campbell, you're a wonderful gentleman. Anyone ever told you that?"

Disbelief. "No, no one ever did."

She broke off the hug so she could see his eyes. "I have one more question. Did you ask William not to see me, to break off tomorrow's date?"

Puzzlement. "No. I only wanted you to know. Why'd you ask?"

"He texted me that our date was off. You had nothing to do with that?" He shook his head. "I'd already decided not to go out with him, but he cancelled first. I want you to know that."

"Why would you break off your date?"

She drew close to watch his eyes. "Two reasons. First, I saw concern in your eyes, for my well-being, not yours. That scared me."

Curiosity. "What's the second reason?"

Ellie smiled and a wonderful warmth filled her. *He knows.* "Haven't you figured that out? Because of you, Henry Campbell and how I'm intrigued with you."

Chapter 13

At his little flat, Henry couldn't sleep. All he could think about was last night... *and Ellie.* The conversation had been a jumble of emotions. When he felt her anger, he assumed it was at him. But he'd been wrong. As Ellie clung to him in the pouring rain, he felt it. Ellie cared for him, too.

Afterwards, they sat on the swing, his arm around her, snuggling as they talked. When it was time to go, he wanted to touch her lips with his, but no. *The first time needs to be special.* This wasn't infatuation or a run of the mill romance. This was once in a lifetime special.

Despite the miles between them, he could feel her in his heart. It was fabulous. Only God knew why Ellie cared, but she did.

Sleep was not on the menu. Henry was still awake when his mobile rang at two-thirty. Sophie.

"Hello?" he answered.

"Henry?"

He could barely understand her.

"Any way you can come over?"

Sophie was always emotional, but something in her voice concerned him. "What's wrong?"

Her crying intensified. "It was horrible. Benjy will never understand. Come over. I need you desperately."

Fear tingled in his chest. "What happened?"

"William."

Anger replaced the fear. "Did William hurt you?"

She cried harder. "I need you, please?"

Henry was already out of bed. "Be there in a jiffy. Do you need a doctor?"

"N-n-no. Come quick." Sophie disconnected.

Henry's heart was in his throat. *Sophie.* He was out the door within thirty seconds. Her apartment was a twenty-minute drive in normal traffic. He made it in six and took the stairs two at a time.

He knocked softly. "Sophie? It's Henry. Let me in."

The door opened immediately. He recoiled at the sight. Sophie was a mess, makeup askew and smeared from crying. Clothes torn and tattered. Her left eye was black and blood was around her nostrils. But her eyes were feral. Like he was looking into the face of a terrified, battered animal instead of his beautiful friend.

Sophie grasped him tightly. "Henry."

She started to collapse, so he swept her into his arms and carried her to the sofa. For half an hour, she cried inconsolably.

Henry was fighting back his anger. "What happened? Did William do this?" She didn't answer, so he gently held her and waited for her reply.

Slowly, she relaxed her grip to look at him.

He brushed the hair from her eyes. "It's all right, I'm here. What happened?"

Sophie sobbed hard. "I did it."

"Did what?"

"I-I asked him to back away from Ellie."

A bitter cold sensation filled him. "He hit you because of that?"

"No. He made me take her place."

God, no. Henry bolted to the water closet and threw up.

She followed him and put her arms around him. "I gave in. It was the only way he would stop."

Henry saw red. William had assaulted Sophie. Everything was blurry as he held his friend. Her tears started again.

"Benjy will hate me now. He'll leave me."

"Where did William do this?"

"His apartment. I gave him what he wanted."

"Why?"

She dried her eyes. "I did it for you. You told me unless I made him stop, our friendship was over. I had no choice. I couldn't lose you. You're the only friend I have left."

Tears stung his eyes. "I never expected you..." He wiped his cheeks. "This is my fault. God, I'm sorry."

She looked away. "No. It's my fault..."

"Why did he hurt you?"

"I couldn't stand it anymore. I told him to stop."

"Did he?"

New tears came from Sophie's eyes. Henry held her tightly while he waited for her reply. It came slowly. "He... he told me to take it... with a stiff upper lip. I tried to stop him, but he hit me over and over... so horrible, so degrading. Benjy won't want me anymore."

This is because of what I said. Dammit! "I think I need to call the police."

Sophie pushed him away. "No, no. I was kind of willing, at first. It got out of hand, that's all." Her hand flew to her mouth. "Help me to the loo, I'm going to be sick."

He carried her into the water closet, closing the door to give her privacy. *Because of my cruelty, you paid the price.* Henry didn't have a clue what to do, but knew who would. He grabbed his mobile and started dialing.

***

The night had been better than a fairy tale. She couldn't fall asleep. *Henry.* Her last glimpse at the clock read 3:00 A.M. *How can I feel him inside my heart like this?*

Her dreams took over. She was walking in a beautiful emerald green forest of fragrant pines under a full moon and starlight so bright she could see the Milky Way. Holding her arm was Henry. Without a word, they shared their thoughts as they strolled. Coming to a knoll overlooking a silvery river, Henry turned and leaned in to kiss her. Just as their lips were about to touch, the sound of her cell interrupted them. The alarm clock read a quarter to five.

"Hello?"

"Ellie, sorry to wake you. I need your help."

His tone brought her to full awareness. "Is everything okay?"

"No." His anger grabbed her heart. Henry told her about Sophie... and William.

"What can I do?"

"Talk to her. This is my fault. I don't know what to say or do."

"I'm on my way."

It was almost six when she knocked on the door. Ellie heard Sophie scream, "Don't answer it. It might be William!"

"I'm here to protect you." Henry opened the door. Ellie squeezed his hand before heading to Sophie.

Sophie's eyes grew wide with fear. "Don't let her in. Isn't it enough she stole Benjy from me? Kick her out."

He turned to face Sophie. "I called Ellie."

Ellie tried to hug her, but Sophie pushed her away. "Leave me alone."

Ellie ignored her, drawing her close. "Shush. You need a friend. I'm here for you."

Sophie protested at first, but Ellie didn't let go. Instead, Ellie drew Sophie into her arms. Sophie cried, but finally returned Ellie's hug.

Ellie kissed her hair. "It's okay to cry, honey. Henry told me what happened."

Still crying, Sophie pushed back to look at Ellie. "What did he tell you?"

"Everything, Sophie, everything."

Sophie's hands covered her face. "I'm sorry. God paid me back for what I did. You'll never forgive me..."

Ellie lifted Sophie's head so they were eye to eye and placed her finger against Sophie's lips. "I forgive you, Sophie. And just so you know, I'm not interested whatsoever in Benjamin. You see, his girlfriend is my best friend. Nothing will ever come between us. I'm here for you now and always will be. I love you, Sophie."

Sophie's tears wet Ellie's shirt. Henry's feelings galloped into her heart. Shock. She knew he didn't understand. Sophie was in the lowest crevice of her life. *I've been there.* Just like Aunt Katie and Uncle Jeremy had been when she needed them, Ellie would be Sophie's rock. *My turn to be strong.*

After Sophie calmed down, the two disappeared into Sophie's room.

Ellie returned alone. Anger filled her heart. Hers and Henry's. "I need you to run an errand," she said to him.

Confusion. "At a time like this, you want me to run an errand?"

Her eyes narrowed. Bitterness flowed from her lips. "That scum drove her home after he was done. Wouldn't give her back her car keys or purse until she 'earns them back'." Ellie calmed herself with a deep breath. "That will not happen."

Henry's anger grew.

"You were a Royal Marine. Go fetch Sophie's things. Somehow, I know you're the man for the job." She knew Henry could read between the lines.

His hatred of William was about to blow. "Be glad to pay the bastard a visit."

Ellie touched his face briefly. Henry had tears in his eyes, but she wasn't sure if they were of anger or sorrow.

He made a fist and held it to his chest. "Be back soon."

Ellie grasped his cheeks so the two of them were looking pupil to pupil. "Henry, please, please, please be safe. Sophie needs you; that you know. But I... I need you, too."

"Worry about him, not me."

Henry turned to the door, but Ellie couldn't let him leave without telling him first. She hugged him and whispered in his ear, "I finally understand. That could have been me. That's why you were so upset."

His green eyes blazed with an intensity she hadn't known existed. Anger and something else. He kissed her cheek and stood at the door. She felt it, undeniably. *Love*.

Out of nowhere, Sophie appeared and wrapped herself around Henry. "I couldn't have survived without you. Hope you know how much I love you."

He kissed her cheek. "Love you too, Soph."

As the words left his lips, he glanced at Ellie. Worry.

Don't be. She smiled and his feelings calmed. "By strength and guile, Henry." The SBS motto. "This one's for Sophie."

There was fire in his eyes. She felt him inside her heart again. *Love you, too, Henry*. The door closed behind him.

Chapter 14

*L*ess than twenty minutes later, a soft knock came to the door. Ellie peeked through the glass. Ben. She opened the door.

He held a large bouquet of flowers. He'd been smiling, but his face sobered when he saw Ellie.

"Why are you here?" he asked. All color left his face. "Is Sophie sick?"

A soft sob came from the couch behind her. "Oh, Benjy."

Ben ran past her to Sophie, but stopped when he saw her face.

"What the...?"

"Sit with me a while." Sophie took his hand and led him to her bedroom.

Ellie put on a pot for tea. Sophie's door flew open and Ben rushed out of the flat. His face was red and his cheeks were wet. He slammed the door behind him.

Sophie stumbled from the room, sobbing uncontrollably.

Ellie ran to her. "What happened?"

She was still sobbing. "I-I-I told him the truth. Start to finish, in detail."

Chills ran over Ellie.

"What did he say?"

Sophie reached for a tissue. "He told me... this was all his fault... and that he loved me... more than ever." Sophie buried her head in her hands.

***

When Henry knocked on the door, it was almost noon. He'd felt Ellie's frantic prayers for his safety all morning. He wanted to call, but he'd left his mobile at the flat. Unfortunately, calls to Sophie's phone went unanswered.

Ellie yanked the door open and leapt into his arms. "I was so worried. Are you okay?"

Ben staggered in behind Henry. "Your Royal Marine's fine. Better than me." He held up his bandaged right hand. "Where's Sophie?"

"Sleeping."

Ben nodded. "Think I'll go watch over her." Ben stared at Sophie's door. "Like I should have been doing all along." He entered Sophie's room and quietly closed the door.

Ellie turned to Henry, inspecting his bruised and bloody knuckles. "Are you okay?"

Now that I'm with you. "Yes. My wounds will heal. Good thing I was there when Benjamin arrived. He was set on killing William."

She drew a sharp breath. "How badly is William hurt?"

"He'll live. By the way, he agreed to leave London... today. Never to return."

"Tell me what happened. From the moment you got there. Leave nothing out," Ellie begged.

Henry told her an abridged version, leaving out the gory details, then nodded his head at the room. "How's Sophie?"

Henry could feel Ellie was concerned about the closeness he and Sophie shared.

"She'll be fine. Ben told her this was because of him, then he told her he loved her. Best medicine she could have gotten."

He studied her eyes. *No secrets, not from you.* "You were concerned when I told Sophie I loved her." He felt her anxiety.

"Not then, but Sophie has told me a lot about the two of you." Ellie's concern deepened. She drew close to read his eyes. "How much do you love her? I need to know." Her hands trembled.

Oh, Ellie. "Sophie's like a sister."

"Was it always like that?" Ellie's emotion was fear.

"No. When I first met her, I wanted more." He could feel Ellie's fear expand. "But I never let those feelings grow. She *was* my best friend." Now he only felt curiosity radiating from Ellie.

"Was?"

"Something happened."

Her hand flew to her mouth. Deep sorrow. "Oh my God. You slept with her."

"Never."

Curiosity. "Then what happened?"

"All my life, I felt somebody was with me, inside my soul. It wasn't Sophie." Henry softly touched her face as he watched her eyes. "Then you came. For the first time, my heart is full. You, you're the one I've been waiting on."

He could feel Ellie's shock, then hopefulness, then remorse. She turned away. "I'm sorry," she said.

"Why?"

"For asking that. For digging deep."

"Don't be. No secrets between us, ever. Everything I have is yours."

She was jittery. "I just needed to know, before..."

"Before what?"

The sadness in those beautiful brown eyes almost made him cry. Worry. "Before I fall in love again. If I give my heart away and it ends... I couldn't take it."

He kissed her fingertips. "It won't happen. I promise."

Warmth. Happiness. The world started to fade. Her eyes were so gorgeous, Henry couldn't wait any longer and leaned in to kiss her. Ellie closed her eyes and moved toward him.

"Hey, you two," Sophie's voice interrupted. "We're starved."

Ellie shot Henry another look. Deep affection, desire. She cleared her throat. "We're hungry, too." Then she whispered loud enough for Henry to hear, "Just not for food."

Chapter 15

As the day progressed, Ellie watched in awe as Ben waited on Sophie, hand and foot. Exactly what her friend needed from the man she loved.

While Sophie took a nap, Ellie and Henry snuggled on the sofa. Henry fell asleep holding her. The lack of sleep took its toll on Ellie and she smiled as she drifted off. *We fit together perfectly.*

Her mind replayed that magical night at Diana's Memorial Garden. Henry had dried her feet before they walked to watch the sunset. The scene slowly changed. Ellie was standing alone at the railing of a ship. Her heart was breaking as she waved goodbye to Henry. He turned from her. Her mother's voice was like fingernails on a chalkboard saying, *"You'll never see him again."*

Ellie bolted awake, jarring Henry.

He immediately took her hands. "What's wrong?"

Her mouth was dry. "It's nothing. Don't worry about it."

Gently, Henry took her chin. "If it bothers you, it *is* my concern. Tell me."

She knew her face was red. She couldn't tell him, not the real truth. "I'm scared William will seek revenge," she lied. "That's all."

Henry wrapped his arms around her. "There's more. Tell me."

How could he know? His feelings came to her. Concern. Care. "It's nothing."

He touched her hair. "No secrets, remember? What is it?"

Okay, there was a curse with this ability to read each other. She couldn't hide a thing. "What will happen when I return to Chicago?" she wondered aloud, still trying to distract him from what she knew would mean the end of this fairytale romance. Anxiety.

"When do you have to go back?" he asked.

Despite trying to control it, her chin quivered. "In a couple of short months." Calmness.

"Then we'll work out a plan, together." The warmth of his green eyes comforted her. "And William? I'll protect you from anything he can do. If you want, I'll come with you or you can stay at my flat. I'll sleep on the couch." He studied her face, and her feelings. "I've waited my entire life for you, Ellie. I promise, on that same life, we'll find a way."

Ellie wrapped her arms around him. Love, hers *and* his. *I've been waiting for you, too.*

***

Henry unlocked her door. The thought of revenge scared her, especially after seeing what William had done to Sophie. But Henry knew William was in no shape to bother anyone for quite a while. He'd made sure of that, even before Ben arrived.

"Can I make you some tea?" he asked Ellie.

"Yes, please. Maybe with chamomile, so I can sleep."

Henry filled the teapot and set it on the stove. "Ben wants to take Sophie away this weekend. Maybe to see Shakespeare's home. He also mentioned Paris. I have some time coming. Would you want to go, too?" Henry wanted to get Ellie away from London for a few days.

"All in one weekend?"

"No, Paris would be a little later." Fear. *Of what?*

"Let's play it by ear." Her hands were trembling when she touched his face. "Sure you don't mind staying here?" *Fear of William.*

"Not at all."

After tea, Ellie said goodnight and headed to her room. Before she had a chance to close her door, Henry felt it. In that short time her fear had multiplied. Henry retrieved the covers and stood in front of her room.

When he knocked, she spoke through the door. "Yes?"

"Wanted to wish you sweet dreams. You're worried. Don't be. I'll sleep outside your door tonight. If you need anything at all, I'm here. 'Night, my love." Peace.

"You, too." She hesitated then added, "My love."

Henry couldn't help himself. He knew he was smiling ear to ear. *You'll walk the forests of my dreams, sweet Ellie.*

***

The rain beating against the windows woke her. She'd feared her dreams would be bad, but instead, they were sweet. Probably because Henry, her protector, slept in the hallway. She'd checked to see if he was still there when she'd woken in the middle of the night. And there he'd been, just as he'd promised. Ellie put on her makeup.

Henry jumped to his feet as soon as her door cracked opened. His red hair was messed up, but his eyes were intense. "Everything okay?"

She touched his nose. "Perfect. You hungry?"

He reached for her hands and it happened again. Bliss. The world departed as they gazed at each other.

Ellie was overcome with the desire to pull him into her room and bolt the door. As soon as the thought came to her, his face reddened.

He released her hands, but held her gaze. "How can any woman look as beautiful as you so early in the morning?"

When you know the truth you won't say that. Ellie playfully poked his chest. "How can one man be as kind as you when he wakes?"

His laughter tickled her soul. Total happiness, hers and his.

After his shower, they dined on muffins and tea. He offered to drive her in to the office, and it suited Ellie because she couldn't imagine being without him. As soon as he dropped her off, she missed him.

Waiting for her in her inbox was a note from Ben.

'El, I'm taking the week off to be with Sophie. Call me if you need anything. Thank you, and Henry, for yesterday. Your boyfriend stopped me from committing murder. Tell him I said thanks.'

My boyfriend? —Yes, *my* boyfriend.
Only my boyfriend? —I don't know, yet.
Liar.

Ellie's second e-mail was from an old friend from high school whose work had brought her into town for a few days. A plan took form in her mind.

***

Henry felt Ellie's presence even before she made it to the lobby. Happiness, anticipation. He was standing, waiting for her as the elevator doors opened. *So beautiful.* Her dimples were out.

"Hi, Henry."

"Good evening, love. How was your day?" He offered his arm and she took it. *So natural.* They talked about her day as they walked to his car.

"You want to eat out. Where would you like to dine tonight?"

Playful. "How do you know that?"

"I felt it."

"Well then, why don't you tell me where I want to go?"

He studied those delightful eyes. "Italian cuisine."

Ellie's mouth dropped open. "How do you do this?"

He just smiled.

"So, you can read my mind, eh?"

"A little, perhaps."

Ellie stopped to breathe in the fragrance of a rhododendron. "I did something sneaky today. Busy Friday night?"

"N-no. Why do you ask?"

She quickly turned to face him. "You tell me."

He again gazed into her eyes. Mischievous. "Special dinner?"

She touched his nose. "Nope."

"Dancing?"

"Maybe later, but that's not it." She started to walk away so he quickly followed.

"What is it?"

Ellie giggled. Joviality. "Thought you could read my mind. Guess a girl does have secrets after all, thank God."

"That's not fair. I'd tell you."

Playful. "I will... as soon as you guess."

"Please tell me."

Once again she turned to face him. Her hand was shaking as she touched his arm. "Were you serious when you said you wanted to know more about me?"

A strong feeling, but he couldn't identify it. "You know I do. I hope you'll tell me everything, in time."

Deep, deep affection was reflecting from her eyes as well.

"I want you to know everything about me. I might have trouble opening up sometimes, but I'll try." The look in her eyes melted his heart. "I don't think I could, or would want to keep anything from you. On Friday, I'll show you something I once was and maybe will be again, someday. I want to share it with you." Her smile changed as she wrinkled her nose.

So secretive. "Some*thing* you once were? What is it?"

"Guess. I thought you could read my mind." The warmth of her hand was driving him insane.

Okay, smarty. Can you tell what I feel about you?

She paled. Near disbelief. Wonder. "I don't understand. What's happening between us?"

"What do you mean?"

Ellie's eyes delved deep into his soul. "This, this... magic. Is it really real? I've never experienced anything like this before."

"I haven't either, but it's the absolute best feeling ever. Like we're one."

Ellie cupped his cheek with her hand, her brown eyes pleading. "Make me a promise."

"Yes?"

"Please, never let this end."

Henry took her hand and kissed her fingers. "As long as I draw breath, I promise it won't."

Chapter 16

Despite asking in every possible way he could think of, Ellie was tight-lipped about Friday. Henry asked her to lunch.

"Can't. I've got plans," she answered.

He pouted, stuck out his bottom lip and made the saddest eyes he could.

Ellie laughed at him. The mystery lady. "Nice try, Henry. You forget I deal with people all day long. Nothing I haven't seen. A little waiting will do you good."

Hmm, I'll try a different approach. "I don't mind the wait, but for all I know, you're having lunch with Prince Harry at the Palace."

She laughed and poured another cup of coffee. Happiness. "You're just trying to get information. Besides, he's married."

"Sure."

Truthfulness. Ellie whispered, "I guarantee you. There's no one else." Kindness. Sudden devilry. She viciously started tickling his ribs. "You're the one surrounded by women all day long. How do I know you aren't just stringing me along while you wait for some rich Duchess to claim you as her own? Um-huh! Maybe I'm the one who should be concerned." Both were laughing as she teased him.

He turned and embraced her. Their laughter stopped. Her lips were so close he could almost taste them. Her breath smelled luscious. Apricots. When their eyes met, the world all but melted away. The depths of those eyes... Henry could almost see her heart and mind. *We're one.* A funny feeling tingled in his chest. He willed it not to stop. At that very moment he needed to kiss her.

Lips against her ear, he whispered, "No woman could ever take your place in my heart. Ellie, I..."

She pushed him away. She was blushing. "Henry Campbell... we can't. Not yet."

"Can't what?" A jumble of emotions. Fear, desire, *and love?* She suddenly turned away. His voice was soft. "I feel it, Ellie."

She didn't face him. "I know you do. But we, we have to leave now."

He turned her toward him. Her warm hands were trembling.

"Did I do something wrong?" he asked.

Her face turned red. Her feelings faded. "No. We just have to get going." She squeezed his hands. "Is what I'm feeling from you real? Please don't play with me."

"Why would you think that?"

"I've been hurt before. If this isn't... what I'm feeling inside, if it's not how you feel, tell me now."

"I'd never play games with you. If you're feelings match mine, this is very real. Do you want me to tell you how I feel?"

She drew a deep breath. "Yes, but not right now. Tonight." She kissed his hand and turned away.

Her feelings were back. And man, were they good!

"I'm going to run upstairs and change. Down in a jiffy."

Henry's gaze lovingly followed her until she was out of sight. Under his breath, Henry muttered, "Don't change too much. You're absolutely perfect. Just the way you are." He packed his things and turned when he heard her heels on the hardwood stairs. He let out a gasp when he caught sight of her. His heart fluttered wildly in his chest. She was wearing a lovely white print dress with yellow roses.

"Oh my goodness, Ellie. You did the impossible."

She stopped abruptly on the bottom step as her smile left her face. "Something wrong?"

"Not at all, but you... Every time I see you, I'm shocked that you look more beautiful than the time before, but this morning, Miss Lucia, you look absolutely exquisite." Her smile and dimples returned. Joy, unbounding joy.

***

For Ellie, the day seemed weeks long. She couldn't wait for this night. Henry's curiosity filled her heart. When she walked into his office, he greeted her with a long hug. She held his hand and led Henry to the Land Rover. Every cell in her body tingled with anticipation. Ever the gentleman, Henry opened the driver's door for her before climbing in the passenger seat.

Ellie's smile awaited him. "How much do you trust me, Henry?"

He answered immediately. "Totally, Ellie, totally."

Opening the console, she pulled out a silk scarf that matched her dress. She teased him with it for a few seconds. "If you don't mind, I'd like to blindfold you." Desire.

He trembled before answering, "I don't mind, at all."

Ellie bit her lip. "This is hard, letting you see the inner me. Before I came to London, I never dreamed I'd open up to anyone, again." Sorrow. Understanding. She squeezed his hands. "Henry, I feel so comfortable, so complete when I'm with you. Like I've known you forever. I promised I'd let you in. Tonight's the beginning of that promise."

"Take all the time you need. I'll always be here."

Her vision blurred. It was right there. She felt it. Unconditional.

"Blindfold me, my lady."

She giggled as she covered his eyes, asking if he was comfortable. She drove for about twenty minutes before parking. The sound of band music wafted in. Curiosity. She climbed out and circled around the vehicle. Opening his door, she firmly grasped one of his hands and guided him out into a standing position, then reached into the backseat to retrieve the picnic basket in her other hand.

Ellie was ever careful with her ward, telling him when to lift his feet high and when to watch his step. They walked while the music grew ever louder.

"Stop." She held his hand for balance. "Sit down, please."

Sophie bounded over and hugged her, then lifted the picnic basket away. "I see you're playing the old blindfold trick on Henry." Sophie's voice was much stronger than the last time they'd spoken. No apprehension, only merriment.

Ellie squeezed Henry's hands. "That's right, Sophie. Make sure he doesn't cheat with the blindfold. Now Henry, when you hear my name over the loud speaker, remove the cloth, but not before. Tonight is not only for you, it's because of you." She pressed her lips to his fingers before letting go.

***

The music was what they called "Big Band" in America. While Ellie had been holding his hands, it had only been background noise. But with her gone, he listened intently. The music reminded him of a steam train moving along the rails. A male voice started singing the words 'Chattanooga Choo Choo'. Henry had never listened to the lyrics before, but now they made him laugh.

The music stopped and a deep voice spoke over the public address system: "Ladies and gentlemen, the United States Navy Jazz Band brings you a special treat this evening. All the way from Savannah, Georgia, I'm pleased to announce our special guest. This charming young lady is a special friend of our lead saxophone and trumpet players. A true Georgia peach. Ladies and gentleman, I present Ms. Eleanor Lucia."

Henry ripped off the scarf to discover he was seated in front of a bandstand. His heart swelled with pride because Ellie, *his Ellie,* was up on the stage holding a trumpet. Next to her stood a tall sailor, also with a trumpet, and a short red-headed lady holding a saxophone and wearing military dress whites. Henry strode forward until he was standing right in front of the bandstand. Total happiness.

The band leader handed Ellie a microphone. "Please do us the honor of introducing the next song, Ms. Lucia."

Her sparkling eyes were on Henry. Honor. Respect. "I'd be glad to, Captain. But first, I want to dedicate this song to my dearest and most cherished friend." She held her hand over the microphone, speaking directly to him. "What's your middle name, Henry?"

At that precise moment in time, Henry couldn't even remember his own name.

Sophie yelled it out instead. "It's Thomas. Henry Thomas Campbell!"

Ellie winked down at him from the stage. Strong, deep affection. "I dedicate this song to my very best friend, Henry Thomas Campbell, formerly of Her Majesty's Royal Marines. This song is for you. Forgive me for playing an American military song when you served Her Majesty, but our countries are the closest of friends, just as you and I are. Ladies and gentlemen, continuing with the Navy's tribute to Glenn Miller, we present, 'American Patrol'. Start us off, Captain."

She turned off the microphone. Hopefulness. Begging him to read between the lines. Henry did. The music started slowly, but within twenty seconds, both trumpet players were blasting out a song he'd never heard before. The tune was merry, but that was nothing compared to seeing his Ellie having the time of her life.

The winds of an approaching storm carried Ellie's scent to him. His heart was ready to beat out of his chest. She was giving him two gifts. The first was the song, but the sweeter gift was that Ellie was revealing her inner self to him. His chest burst with pride and something else. With the greatest intensity in his entire life. He knew exactly what that feeling was. Henry was in love with Ellie. He wanted to be with her, cherish and love her, not just tonight but forever.

Ellie winked at him as she played. Henry sent prayer after prayer of thanksgiving to God for sending Ellie into his life. Love. And *her* love was the greatest gift he'd ever received.

On stage, Ellie kept playing her heart out. But while her hands were on the trumpet, her eyes were glued to Henry. His heart swelled so big his chest could hardly contain it. She played perfectly, hitting every note. When the song climaxed, everyone in the crowd stood, giving Ellie and the American Navy Band a standing ovation.

Chapter 17

Henry was waiting as Ellie walked down the stairs from the bandstand. She reached for him and they embraced tightly. The feel of his lips against her ear turned her on, immensely.

"I'm so proud of you, Ellie," he whispered. "Thank you. You don't know how much this night means to me."

She pulled back so they could look into each other's eyes. "I know exactly what this means to you."

He raised his eyebrows. "You do?"

She smiled wider, wrinkling her nose at him. "Remember the other day when you walked into the Bistro and told me you could feel me there?" He nodded. "On stage tonight, I felt something of the same thing... like you were inside my heart. Like we're one."

"I felt it, too. One heart, two bodies. You can read my feelings? I want to see how well you know me." Hopefulness that she knew.

Her body tingled. "God help me if I'm wrong. I'd be so embarrassed."

"Go on."

His essence curled into her senses. She breathed deeply before continuing. "When you saw me up on stage, several things came to your mind. First was disbelief that I was really letting you in, because you weren't sure I ever would. Then thankfulness because I had drawn the curtain back, like I promised. Am I right so far?"

In a voice barely louder than a whisper, he answered, "Precisely. You read me perfectly."

Her cheeks heated. "But something stronger poured into me. Was there more?" He slowly nodded. "Henry, I felt like, well, I'm so scared to say this."

"Tell me."

She stared for a long moment. As many times before, everything faded away. She knew her eyes were welling. His were glistening. Ellie drew a deep breath. "Henry, I think I felt you, well..." she paused for a second, "...it was like you realized you love me." The intensity of the heat in her face increased. "I can't believe I said that. If I was wrong..."

Henry smiled and placed his forefinger over her lips. Joy. Amazement. Total love. He drew her close.

"Ellie, you weren't wrong. I am in love with you. Have been since before I knew your name on that boat. You read my mind perfectly. My exact thoughts. Now, in return, may I tell how you felt?"

She was crying and laughing now. She'd gone out on a thin limb, and much to her surprise, that skinny branch hadn't broken off. *Henry loves me!* Two weeks ago, she would never have imagined a closeness like she shared with this Scotsman, nor would she have had the courage to say the things she just did.

His green eyes were ablaze. The feelings swirling around in her head and chest were becoming clearer now. *God, please, please let Henry be the one you intended for me!*

Ellie cleared her throat. "Okay. Tell me what I felt."

"Several distinct feelings. First, this was hard for you. To open up. You wanted to give me a special gift, one you hoped I'd love and appreciate, which I do. The last thing I felt was..." Henry's eyes shined. "The last thing I felt was that you're falling in love with me, too."

She let out a happy sob as she grasped him tightly. The band started playing another song. She pulled back and gazed into his eyes. Ellie could truly see it. *Henry really loves me!*

"This is my favorite song, of all time. 'Moonlight Serenade'. Please dance with me."

Happiness beyond measure. "I'd be honored!" Henry beamed. He placed his arms around her waist and she linked her arms around his neck.

As they danced, Ellie sang to him, softly. *Never known this feeling before...* Henry leaned forward, softly kissing her forehead, then kissing her left cheek. Ellie burst out laughing.

Confusion. "Did I do something wrong?"

She shook her head. "No, I suddenly thought of my Aunt Kaitlin. Often, when Jeremy kisses her, she'll say, 'Please sir, I'd like another'. They have a perfect love."

Her body trembled with anticipation. Henry's green eyes were smiling, beckoning her to kiss him. *So handsome. So majestic. My prince.* She couldn't wait one second longer.

"Please sir, may I have another? But this time, two inches to the left." His smile made her giddy. She bit her lip. "Let's pick up with what you wanted to do this morning. I believe you were just about to..."

Henry didn't wait for her to finish. His lips slowly and softly touched hers. So sweet. So soft. She'd entered heaven. The world disappeared. Nothing else mattered. The storm finally arrived, drenching them with rain. Neither noticed. Their first kiss went on and on. She pulled away to catch her breath, but together, they again joined their lips with urgency. This kiss lasted even longer. Kiss after kiss followed. She couldn't get enough. He couldn't either.

Neither noticed when the band, safely sheltered under the roof of the bandstand, moved on to 'In the Mood'. Everyone in the park was laughing as Ellie and Henry slowly swayed back and forth in the pouring rain.

Over Henry's shoulder, Ellie saw Ben approaching, an open umbrella in his hand, a dumb smile on his face. First he covered the two of them and then tucked the umbrella handle into one of Ellie's hands behind Henry's neck. When he sauntered back toward Sophie, Ellie immediately realized that she and Henry were the center of attention.

Who cares? Her lips found his again. Bliss. Everlasting bliss.

After another band number concluded, they slowly broke off their latest kiss. Henry's look turned her on so much. *Is this a dream?*

He'd read her mind. His next words confirmed it. "This is real. I love you, Ellie."

Her throat tightened. Ellie wanted to tell him, but both times she'd confessed her love, her heart had been broken. What if they drifted apart? *I'd lose my mind. I just can't say it.*

Henry kissed her again. "You don't need to say it. I feel it."

"I do, too. It just might take a while to say it out loud, but I do."

His eyes smiled at her. "I don't care if it takes a hundred thousand years. I already feel it, and you, in my heart."

Is this real? Doubt nagged at Ellie's soul. "Suppose you get tired of waiting and leave me?" Warmth.

"I can promise you that will never happen. I'm in love with you, Ellie, forever."

***

Ellie was glad they were getting away after such an eventful week. She and Ben were lucky to have Henry and Sophie as both professional and private tour guides. They'd piled into Ellie's Land Rover and the first stop was Stonehenge. Sophie and Henry alternated historical comments as they passed through the beautiful English countryside. In the early afternoon, they reached Stratford-upon-Avon, Shakespeare's home. Sophie looked worn out, so Henry and Ellie dropped the pair off at the hotel and they all agreed to meet at six for dinner.

In the meantime, Henry took Ellie to a quaint English tea room on the second floor of a charming old house close to Shakespeare's home. They were enjoying each other's company when Henry said, "Love, please tell me what you are thinking."

She smiled. How could he read her so well? "How do you know I'm thinking anything?"

He kissed her hand. "Because there is such a connection between us. Pardon me for saying this, but remember how I told you I always felt there was someone there with me during my childhood?"

She gazed into his green eyes. "Yes, I remember it, vividly."

"I no longer feel that way. Instead, that person is sitting right across from me. Do you feel that way, too?"

So much love. "Yes, I do. I've never felt this way. We have a special connection. I tried to figure it out, but it defies explanation. You're in my mind and my heart... and Henry? Never let it stop. I told you about my life. Before I came here to England, my life was so unsure, like I was just a spectator. But now, I feel so alive, almost like the first time ever. I, uh..." She hesitated, allowing her voice to trail away.

Understanding. "I love you, too, Ellie. Now, tell me what's on your mind. Something precious, isn't it?"

"Yes, yes it is. Kaitlin is flying in on Friday. Jeremy is returning from Scotland. They're heading to Paris for a long weekend, then on to Venice for a week. They invited me to go along with them." She hesitated momentarily. "Will you come with me?"

Sorrow. "I'd love to, Ellie, but I can't get that much time away. I only have a couple days of holiday saved up. I could possibly come to Paris, but not Venice. You should go, though. I've never been there, but I hear it's quite beautiful."

She shook her head. "No, I won't go to Venice either. Our time is limited as it is. We'll do Paris, but not Venice. I don't want to go there without you."

Puzzlement. "Why? You should go."

Her mouth was dry. "This is happening so fast... Henry, in you I've found everything I ever wanted or dreamed of. I want to see Venice, but only on one condition."

Confusion. "What's that?"

"I need to explain something." She held his hands tightly. So warm. "I don't understand why I feel so comfortable talking about everything with you, especially my feelings. But I want you to know all of my feelings, my intentions. I was hurt badly by both Ben and Steve, so saying I love you is going to take a while. But Henry, I feel it and you know I do, too, don't you?" Yes, he did. "Wait for it to come out and don't give up on me. I think you're my soul mate, the one I want to share life with. That's my secret prayer. That we're meant to be together forever."

She stopped to wipe her cheeks. Tonight will be the test, when you find out...

"Maybe it'll happen," she continued, "but maybe it won't. I hope and pray it does. But until we know it for sure, I don't want to squander or waste any memories. The only way I want to see Venice is with you."

Disbelief. He stood up and hugged her. "I'll wait forever for you to say it, but I know how you feel. As plain as the smile on your face. But I won't wait one second longer to say it to you. Wait. What's your middle name?"

She pulled away. "You might not like it. So old fashioned." Anticipation. *Here goes.* "My full name is Eleanor Faye Lucia."

"Faye," he murmured, savoring the sound of it on his tongue. "The name is beautiful, just like you. I can tell you now. With all my heart and soul, not only do I love you, Eleanor Faye Lucia, but I am hopelessly and forever in love with you." His lips met hers.

***

They picked up Ben and Sophie and went to dinner. As they ate, Henry felt something bothering Ellie, very badly. After returning back to the hotel, they took a walk to watch the sun set. At a wall bordered by wildflowers, Henry held her. Ellie trembled at his touch.

He softly kissed her hair. "Ellie?"

It was as if she had just come out of a trance. "Yes, Henry?"

"I know what's bothering you."

She looked away. "I'm afraid you don't have a clue." Her eyes didn't meet his. Regret. Sorrow.

Very gently, he grasped her chin, turning her head slowly until her eyes looked into his. Those eyes were troubled. "It'll be okay. I understand."

She looked away. "No, no you don't."

He again lifted her chin to bring their eyes together. He smiled with understanding. "Tonight's the first night we'll share a room together. We have separate beds. Or if you're uncomfortable with that, I'll just get another room."

Her eyes clouded. Embarrassment? "It's not that. I'm looking forward to sleeping next to you."

Now he was puzzled. He was so sure he'd read her mind, but now he was concerned. "You can trust me. What's in that pretty little head of yours?"

Horror. She bit her lip as she looked at him. "I hope I'm worrying over nothing. You're so special. I care about you so much, but I'm scared."

Her hands trembled inside his. "Scared?"

She looked away, "This is so hard. I don't know how to say it, so I'll blurt it out. Our relationship is like nothing I've ever known. You know about Steve and Ben. I never cared how they saw me, but you? How you see me matters a lot."

Concern. "When I look at you..."

"Stop for a second, okay? This is difficult. Don't interrupt me. You said you wanted to know everything. If that's what you want, you get the good and the bad. This is important to me." Tears started to fill her eyes. "Henry, you mean the world to me. When you see me with nothing on, I'm afraid you'll be appalled."

His eyes opened wide. "Just because we're sharing a room doesn't mean we'll be naked."

Modesty. She blushed deeply. "No, you don't understand. I wasn't talking about seeing me with my clothes off. That may come in time, but that won't happen tonight."

Henry was confused. "I've no idea what you're talking about."

Ellie's tears were flowing freely now. Such sadness. Henry's heart went out to her. All the happiness and confidence she'd appeared to have earlier now abandoned her.

"When I was a teenager, I had a really bad case of acne," she said. "You see how much makeup I use. I wear it thickly to cover up the scars. I'm afraid when you see me without all that makeup, the sight will make you sick. I'm afraid you'll walk out on me."

Henry jumped off the wall, grabbing her tightly. "Never. In my eyes, you're beautiful. Always will be. It wasn't your beauty that attracted me to you."

"Then what was it?"

He brushed her tears away, "That's easy. Two things, actually. The warmth of your eyes and that engaging smile of yours. One look and baby, I was hooked. I hope you realize our love flows two ways. I want you to know everything about me, too. Please don't think I'm so shallow that I only care about your pretty face and your hot body."

Even though her eyes were still moist, her dimples made an appearance. "Do you really think I have a hot body?"

"Is the Pope Catholic? Ellie, in my eyes, you are absolutely perfect."

***

Despite their earlier conversation, Ellie was self-conscious as she walked out of the bathroom. Void of makeup, she held a towel over her face, exposing only her eyes. It would have been easier to walk out naked. Henry watched her, his sadness showing. She'd explained how her mother said the scars made her look ugly and revolting. All she ever wanted was her mother's approval, but she never got it. Time and again, her mother ran her down.

Henry's anger flashed through when she told him. Life was tough not only being the eldest, but also the least favorite child. She'd wanted her parents' love, but never got it.

"When the bottom of my world dropped out—when Steve abandoned me—all Mom did was criticize. In fact, she turned her back on me. If not for Aunt Kaitlin and Uncle Jeremy, I wouldn't have survived."

Henry held her. "I'll make it a point to personally thank them."

Ellie's eyes were moist as she stood in front of him. She squeezed them shut tightly in prayer.

"You'll always be beautiful to me," Henry whispered.

She couldn't let go of the face towel. Henry gently tugged at it. Slowly Ellie released her grip. The towel fell to the floor. She knew her acne scars were deep, ugly and plentiful. *So hideous.* She searched his eyes. He smiled momentarily before his lips turned into a deep frown.

He hates me. Ellie felt his change of emotions. She slowly backed away. "Oh my God, you're appalled! I knew it! You hate me!" Tears filled her eyes.

He kissed her lips quickly. "You misinterpreted me. I love you and nothing will ever change that. You're still the most beautiful girl I've ever seen. Yes, you have scars. So what? I love you so much. They're beauty marks to me. Forgive me for what you felt. It isn't directed at you. I'm mad at your mother. She must be off her rocker to ever think you were anything but gorgeous. I might not be able to contain my anger if I ever meet her."

Total love. Understanding. Ellie jumped into his arms. "Oh, Henry!" She sobbed as he held her. His lips found hers many, many times before they fell asleep on separate beds, hands reaching across the chasm. Ellie slept peacefully, content in Henry's love.

Chapter 18

After an uneventful transatlantic flight, Kaitlin was glad to be reunited with her husband Jeremy. Her niece had the London operation well under control, removing any possible reason not to follow their weekend plans. Kaitlin and Jeremy took their seats on the Euro-Star high speed train bound for Paris. Sophie, Ben, Ellie and Henry had seats across from each other down the aisle.

Kaitlin and Jeremy held hands. Jeremy softly kissed Kaitlin's brow. "I missed you so much. I love you."

"I love you, too." Kaitlin felt her lips curl into a smile. "It appears quite a change has come over Ellie. Have you noticed it? She looks so different. I haven't seen her without makeup since she was in grade school. Even from this distance, you can plainly see the scars on her face. She was always self-conscious about them. What happened while you were over here?"

"Not sure, but I think she's in love. See how comfortable and happy she looks? An air of self-confidence she lacked before." They watched as Ellie suddenly turned, kissing Henry.

Kaitlin laughed. "Yep, no doubt about it. Our little girl's in love. What do you think of Henry? Meet him before today?"

"Yes. Just before I left for Scotland. He had a girlfriend. She was weird."

"Ellie told me about her. Heidi. But they've broken up. I met Henry today at lunch. I really like that boy. Don't know why, but I feel like I've known him for some time. You still didn't answer me though. What do you think of him?"

"He's a good man, former Royal Marine. The day I met him, we spent an hour talking. Honorable, kind, caring. He sees something in Ellie, but more importantly, Ellie found something wonderful in him. In all these years I've never seen her so happy. You're right. She's in love."

Kaitlin kissed her husband. "I believe you hit the nail on the head. But realize, she isn't the only girl in this family who's in love. After all, I'm in love with you. Have I told you that today?"

He smiled that crooked smile she loved so very much. "Many times. The first time was before you whispered a word. It came through loud and clear. I love you, Katie, forever."

***

Ellie was tired when they arrived at the hotel late in the evening. After registration, they agreed to meet for breakfast at eight. Ellie and Henry were holding hands as they exited the elevator. Henry squeezed her hand. Happiness. "Thanks for asking me along. Paris is always beautiful, but it pales in comparison to you." He wrapped his arms around her and their lips melted together.

Her head was spinning. "Thank you. This means so much, you being here." She inserted her key card into the door. "I'm so excited..."

Her thoughts were immediately interrupted. There was a problem. A big problem. Instead of two twin beds as promised, a king-sized bed dominated the room.

While she and Henry had slept in the same room before, they'd never shared a bed. *I'm not ready for that.*

Henry picked up on her feelings. "I'll talk with reservations. We'll switch rooms, okay?"

Understanding. "Would you mind?" Ellie asked. She didn't know whether to be embarrassed by her reaction, or relieved that Henry was so understanding.

"Back in a jiffy." He kissed her before heading to the lobby. But he wasn't smiling when he returned. "I've bad news. The hotel is completely booked. If you still aren't wild about sharing a bed, I'll find another hotel."

Ellie shook her head. "No. We'll figure something out."

"I could sleep on the floor," Henry offered.

Hopefulness. "You'd be uncomfortable, Henry. That seems ridiculous. In fact I feel ridiculous even talking about this. It's not that I don't want to sleep with you. It's just, well..."

He smiled softly at her. "You aren't ready to make love."

She searched his eyes, slowly nodding. "I'm sorry."

Joy. From just being with her. "Don't be. We both want this to be a long-term relationship, not just a bunch of naughty times where we get carried away."

She knew he saw the agreement in her eyes.

"Listen closely," he said. "Our love is something special and precious. I don't want to mess this up. I'd rather wait—running the risk that we never make love—than to do it and have regrets later."

Pure love. "You're special, Henry Thomas Campbell. Did I ever tell you that?"

Amusement. Good as his word, he found a blanket and extra pillow in the closet and spent the night on the floor next to her. Their fingers intertwined as they drifted off.

***

Henry held Ellie's hand when the three couples toured Paris. Sophie acted as their tour guide because she'd been there many times before. They saw Notre Dame, the Louvre, and the Arc de Triomphe before taking an early evening boat ride on the Seine.

Ben had been acting strangely all afternoon. Henry mentioned it to Ellie, she had readily agreed. Ben wasn't himself. As the sun set, the six of them dined on the lower level of the Eiffel Tower, watching the lights of Paris unfold before them. They were preparing to head off in different directions until Ben stood awkwardly, raising his practically untouched wine glass to offer a toast. Henry noted how badly his hand was shaking.

"My friends, thank you for sharing your time in Paris with Sophia and me. Before we part, please join us at the very top of the tower."

Anxiety. Ellie spoke up. "I don't do heights. I'm queasy already. We'll pass on this one. Okay, Henry?" He smiled and nodded at Ellie.

Ben shot Henry a look of desperation. He stepped over and whispered just loud enough for Ellie and Henry to hear. "I need you to come with us. If you do, I promise I'll never ask for anything again, please?"

Ellie and Henry shared a look of curiosity. It suddenly dawned on Henry what Ben was plotting. "Ellie, I changed my mind. I want to see Paris from the top of the Tower."

Fear. "I don't know, Henry. I'm really scared of heights."

He leaned in and whispered, "I think Benjy is going to propose to Sophie. We should be there for her."

She pulled away, eyes wide. "Are you sure?"

"I think so."

Ellie looked at Ben, then Sophie, who was wearing a short black dress and pearls, the vision of beauty. She appeared to be clueless as to what Henry thought Ben had in mind.

Ellie cleared her throat. "Okay, just this once."

Ben shot them both a radiant smile then turned to Jeremy and Kaitlin. "Will you join us?"

Kaitlin smiled. "Of course. I need to be kissed at the top." She winked at Jeremy.

It was obvious something was afoot.

They waited for the crowd to die down so all six of them could ride the elevator together. As soon as they stepped off onto the platform at the top, Henry saw one of the Tower Docents nod at Ben and point to a basket. All three couples enjoyed the breathtaking panorama while Sophie held Ben's hand. They slowly viewed all four directions over the city.

Henry saw Ben release Sophie's hand and remove something from his pocket. Sophie was so engrossed she didn't notice Ben kneel behind her. But the other two couples saw it and waited in anticipation.

Sophie turned her head to say something to her Benjy, but when he wasn't by her side she turned to find him. That's when she saw Ben on one knee, holding out a beautiful solitary diamond engagement ring. Sophie inhaled sharply. Her face turned pale as her hands covered her mouth. Tears ran from her eyes.

Ben smiled at her. "Sophia, we're in the most beautiful, romantic place in the entire universe. But to me, it doesn't compare to your beauty. My life's not worth living without you. I love you so much. Please share your life with me, not only as a friend and lover, but as my wife. Will you marry me?"

Sophie opened her mouth. Nothing came out but sobs. She nodded her head vigorously and reached for his hands. Ben stood and clung to her.

"I love you, Sophie."

Happy emotions engulfed his friend. Henry felt his own heart almost bursting at such a romantic gesture. All Sophie could do was cry and hold Ben tightly.

After watching Ben's proposal, Kaitlin and Jeremy kissed.

Ellie and Henry had also watched the drama unfold, but Ellie's reaction hadn't been what Henry had expected. Extreme sadness. In fact, Ellie had tears in her eyes—and they didn't seem like tears of joy for her friend. Henry had wanted to kiss her, but needed to understand what was going on. Did she still have feelings for Ben? Maybe even love? Before he could do anything, Ellie turned and kissed Henry deeply. Pulling back, she looked into his eyes and said it for the first time. "Henry, I love you!"

Before either could continue, Sophie was there, hugging both of them. Sophie kissed Henry on both cheeks and showed him the ring. She held Ellie. "I know you said what's past is past, but I need to say this. I was so scared of you. Thought you were going to take him from me. But Ben told me you were the one who opened his eyes, made him realize he loved me. Tonight was only possible because of you. I love you, Ellie, so much. Will you be my maid of honor?"

Ellie sniffed and replied, "I'd be honored."

Ben was there next, sweeping Ellie off her feet with a bear hug. "Ellie, you were right. If I'd let Sophie go, I would have cursed myself forever. Can't thank you enough." He kissed Ellie's cheek before shaking Henry's hand, thanking him for being there.

Sophie and Ben turned their attentions to Jeremy and Kaitlin, who were still embracing. Henry held Ellie.

"What's wrong? Something's bothering you. Are you upset because you watched Ben propose to Sophie? You loved him once. Be honest. Do you wish he'd proposed to you instead?"

Ellie shook her head violently. "Henry, that's not it. Do you remember that night at the dock along the Thames?" He nodded. "I knew I was in love with you that night. The thing that makes me sad is..." She gripped his forearms. "The thing that upsets me... in a couple of short weeks, I'm going back to America. I wish that was you and me right now. I can't bear the thought we'll have to leave each other. I've lost two men I loved, but what I felt for them is nothing like what I feel for you. You're the love of my life. I love you so much, Henry." She buried her head against his shoulder.

The basket contained champagne and Jeremy wasted no time popping the cork and pouring for everyone. They enjoyed a glass in celebration.

That night, and every night afterwards, Henry and Ellie slept in each other's arms. They didn't make love, but instead enjoyed the delight of holding each other as they walked in dreams of rapture.

Chapter 19

*T*he earthy scent of rain-soaked Scotland wafted in the car window. Ellie was on cloud nine as they drove to meet Henry's family.

"It's so beautiful here. Did you miss it when you were in the Royal Marines?"

Pride. Honor. "I was in 43 Commando, based out of Clyde, when I wasn't deployed. Clyde's just down the road. That's where I earned my Green Beret."

"Green Beret? Isn't that an American thing?"

Henry laughed. "Similar. I earned mine for passing commando training."

"Wait. You're Scottish. Aren't the Royal Marines part of the British Army?"

"All part of the UK. And the Marines are part of the Royal Navy."

Henry had fulfilled his promise to share everything. *I'm the official expert on you now, Henry.* She kissed his hand. Love. Tenderness. They openly spoke of a future together, and now it was time for action. "I want you to come to America with me," she said with more conviction than she felt. What real incentive did he have to leave this beautiful country?

She stole a glance. His smile was dazzling. Devotion. Love. Happiness. "My contract ends in April," he replied immediately. "I've a substantial bonus coming. I'll need it, you know. Worked too hard and long to miss this payday. That money will let me buy my ticket to visit you."

Ellie's heart dropped. He'd said visit. "Yep. Flights are expensive."

He squeezed her hand. "Sorry about needing the money. I'll join you in April."

Can't wait that long. "Need it? For what?"

"For all the things we'll need as man and..." He stopped to look at her.

Ellie's heart rose higher than the tallest mountain. She sighed happily. "Wife?"

Henry squeezed her hand. "Yes, as my wife. Together, forever and always."

Euphoria, hers and his. *Thank you, God!*

Henry turned his little car down a dirt lane. Ellie's chest and arms tingled. "Do you think they'll..."

He kissed her fingers. "They'll love you, but not as much as I do."

He stopped the car and set the brake. The farm really wasn't much to look at. The property was small but well cared for. Surrounding the house were several small animal sheds and one large barn. The most beautiful thing about the farm was the hedgerows. They provided bright green contrast to the fields of green and brown, as well as the off-white color of the sheep. Charming and beautiful.

Before the engine stopped, a woman ran to the car. She was wide, with graying reddish hair and brilliant green eyes. She hugged her son briefly before racing around the vehicle and crushing Ellie in her arms. She squeezed so hard that Ellie wondered if she'd ever catch her breath again. When the woman released her, Ellie saw stars.

"Henry's told me about you. Name's Darcy, but call me Mum."

"Pleased to meet you... um... Mum."

The stars slowly faded and Ellie's eyes focused. Two men and a beautiful fair-headed girl stood before her, all maybe in their late teens or early twenties. Without a doubt, they were Henry's siblings.

"These are my brothers, Harry and Edmund. And this," he took the girl's hand, "is my baby sister, Margaret."

Margaret's smile was ear to ear, watching as Edmund leaned in to give Ellie a kiss on each cheek. But instead he grabbed Ellie's neck and planted his mouth over hers.

Henry grabbed his brother by his collar and yanked him away. "Behave, Edmund, or I'll whip you."

After that scuffle, Harry only kissed her hand, but didn't say anything. His light brown eyes welcomed her nonetheless.

Margaret, however, engulfed her in a hug almost as big as Darcy's. "So happy another female's here. Been looking forward to meeting you. Welcome home."

Henry's family treated her like a princess, hanging on her every word. Darcy and Margaret provided a light salad for lunch.

After the meal, Henry asked Ellie to walk with him. Something was on his mind, but she didn't know what. In silence, they strolled to the top of a knoll overlooking a neighboring farm. It looked like it hadn't been used for years. The fields were fallow and Ellie could see young trees already taking over.

Henry sniffed, hard. Sorrow. When she glanced his way, she could see the tears streaming down his face. In a flash Ellie remembered the story he had shared... the abandoned farm... and suddenly realized where they were. She held him tightly.

"This farm, it's where Annie lived, isn't it?"

"Yes."

"She was very special, wasn't she?"

He wiped his eyes, voice barely a whisper. "This is where Annie lived with her family. After she died, they couldn't stay here anymore though they refused to sell it because they believed her spirit still walks here. I agree. But you must think I'm crazy."

Regret. "I believe you. You loved her."

He shed a few more tears. "I knew Annie since she was a baby. We played together all the time. Our farms were remote so we became best friends. In secondary school, I fell for a girl named Kara who was beautiful in a physical way that Annie wasn't. When Kara left for university, my heart was broken. When Annie tried to cheer me up, suddenly it dawned on me. I didn't actually want Kara. I wanted the girl who lived one farm over. I'd already fallen in love with her."

The sound of sheep baaing at each other drifted over the hill. Henry turned to Ellie. "Until I met you, I'd never known love like that. We planned our future, six children. Even picked out names. Everything was falling into place. Then one day, her parents went out visiting. Annie was supposed to come over and meet me after chores, but she never arrived. I searched everywhere for her. The house was empty. I looked for almost an hour before I found her. She'd been collecting eggs. I found her, crushed under one of those big round bales of hay, dying."

Henry stopped to clear his eyes. Ellie touched his cheek. He pointed to a spot behind the barn. "No one could ever explain how it fell on her, but it did. I tried, but couldn't move it off her. I called for help, but by the time they arrived, she was gone. I..." He couldn't go on.

Ellie gently wiped away his sorrow.

"I... c-couldn't stay here after her death. So I joined the Royal Marines to get away, but they sent me back here to Clyde. I'd like to visit her grave if you don't mind. I'll hurry back. Just want to say hello." His face was soaked.

Ellie felt his pain. *You need me.* "I'll join you," she said.

"I'd like that." Hand in hand, they walked to Annie's grave. Though the farm wasn't taken care of, the area around her grave was neatly manicured. Flowers were wilting in a vase on the headstone.

Henry touched the marker. "Hello, Annie. Sorry I don't come around like I should. Miss you so much." Henry grew silent.

Ellie spoke softly. "Annie. I wish I'd known you because of what you mean to Henry. Thanks for the love you gave him and... for just being you. I pray we'll meet someday."

Henry hugged Ellie tightly, but didn't speak. They began the walk back across the fields. When the farm was no longer visible, Henry spun Ellie toward him and kissed her softly. The salty taste of his tears lingered on her lips.

"It means so much, you being with me." He brushed the hair from her eyes. "When Annie died, I was inconsolable. But even then, I knew someone was with me, inside. At her grave just now, I felt it again. You. It was you all along. You're in my heart, my soul. You're so much more than the girl I love. God brought us together for something very special, Ellie Lucia."

Unimaginable euphoria. "This is more than love, if such a thing exists."

He kissed her again, then cleared his throat. "I haven't officially proposed, but you do know I intend to marry you, don't you?"

Heaven's doors were opening. Ellie nodded.

"I don't think I can wait any longer. I want to tell my family we're getting married, may I?"

She should be nervous or scared or something. But happiness and love surrounded her. His lips were warm and wet. With scarcely a moment's pause she answered, "I'd be delighted if you told *our* family."

The rest of the walk was light hearted, punctuated every few feet by deep kisses.

The hearty scent of lamb stew greeted them.

Margaret stuck out her lip. "Thanks, Henry. Another woman besides Mum walks in the door, but you keep her all to yourself. What kind of brother are you? You're supposed to take care of me."

She suddenly faced them with her hands on her hips. "What were you doing, anyway? Your faces are flushed." Her mouth fell open. "You two were naughty!"

Ellie knew her own face was red, but she couldn't help laughing.

Darcy hissed at Margaret. "Mind your manners, lass. If you give Miss Ellie such a hard time, she'll never come back and then you'll have even more to complain about."

***

Henry loved the good natured ribbing. Margaret stood to clean off the table.

"Sit down, Margaret," he said. "The dishes can wait." He reached over and squeezed Ellie's hand. Her warmth gave him strength. "Mum, Margaret, Harry, Edmund. We've something we want to share." He could sense Ellie's feelings were happiness, excitement. The women's eyes grew wide. His brothers looked on with envy.

Henry cleared his throat. "When I met Ellie, my life changed. I knew I'd found the woman I, uh..." He suddenly hesitated. *I'm cheating her. No ring on her finger.* He looked down at the table in frustration.

Ellie's angelic voice picked up where he'd failed. "We realized how wonderful it was to be together. I love your son and brother very much, like he loves me. Henry

136

hasn't officially proposed, but we are getting married. We just wanted you, our family, to be the first to know."

Henry stared at her in shock. So brave, so eloquent. Full of happiness. Total silence. His family was stoic. *Disbelief?* Suddenly, they jumped up as one. His brothers fought to be the first to hug her. Harry kissed her cheeks, but Edmund stole another kiss from her lips.

Darcy could wait no more and finally pushed her sons aside, grasping Ellie firmly. "My daughter."

Henry felt Ellie. Wonder. Joy. Love.

Margaret waited her turn with more patience than Henry would have expected. Then his kid sister grabbed Ellie by both hands and swung her around in a circle, head back, laughing as they twirled. They spun around until they both fell laughing to the floor.

Margaret kissed her cheek. "All my life, I prayed for a sister. My prayers have finally come true. You're the sister I dreamed about. May I come visit you in America?"

Henry couldn't believe the reaction. He had to lift Ellie—now in a daze—from the floor and give his sister a gentle shove. With merriment in his voice, he scolded her. "Couldn't you wait five minutes before imposing on Ellie's hospitality?"

Margaret frowned. "It's not fair. You get her all the time. I've wanted a sister forever. I want to spend time with her."

Edmund appeared with a bottle of whiskey. "Celebration!" he shouted and began filling glasses.

Henry felt it. Ellie's immediate discomfort. He knew where it came from.

"That's not a good idea. Can you get Ellie some juice instead?"

Darcy grabbed her cheeks. "Gracious Lord. You have a wee one in the oven!"

Margaret gasped audibly.

Edmund's eyes became even rounder than they'd been before. "You lucky bugger, Henry."

Shock. Ellie's eyes also opened wide. "What?"

"Are you with child, lassie?" Darcy asked.

"N-no. I just don't drink whiskey," Ellie said, suddenly flushed.

Darcy's disappointment showed. "For a moment, I thought *my* prayers were answered."

Chapter 20

They stayed as late as they could before heading back to London. Ellie rested her head on Henry's shoulder. His scent, so masculine, divine. The weekend? Magical. And Henry? He appeared happier than ever.

Darcy kissed her goodbye. "I love you, daughter." Henry's family was amazing. So much love. Ellie's heart was overflowing. *Life's perfect.*

The ringtone caught her attention. It was from the personal cell phone that Ellie kept for emergencies. She hadn't used it since coming to the UK. Her mother's number popped up on caller ID. Fear spiraled up Ellie's spine. *Mom hasn't talked to me in two years.*

"Mom? Is everything okay?"

The voice was icy. "Eleanor. I tried to reach you on the other phone, but I guess you were too busy. Am I interrupting you sleeping with some new man you don't know?"

"What?"

"You slut! How dare you! After the e-mail you sent out, begging for partners, calling yourself 'The Hottest Tramp in London'. Keeping count of how many men you've done. You're a disgrace to this entire family. I should find it hard to believe you've had sex with hundreds of men and brag about it? But somehow I don't. You're just a filthy whore."

Ellie's throat was closing. "Mom, I don't understand."

"The e-mail you just sent. I'm sure you remember. Dirty pictures of you in action, asking who wants to be next."

Henry pulled to the side of the road. Concern.

"Slut!" her mother shouted.

Ellie's stomach was turning. "Mom, I have no idea what you're talking about. I didn't send any e-mails. In fact I don't even have my computer with me."

"Then explain how a naked picture of you doing... *things* with those men arrived in my e-mail. And the website? www.EllieLucialovesto... No, I won't lower myself to even say it. You ugly whore!"

The phone hummed. "Mom. It's Jeremy calling. Call you back in a little while?"

"Don't bother," the older woman huffed. Then the line went dead.

Ellie answered her phone, "Hello?" No answer. She dropped it onto her lap.

Henry reached out to grasp Ellie's hand. "What happened?" he asked.

"I... I don't know." Her cell phone rang again. "Hello?"

"Ellie, are you okay?" Jeremy practically shouted.

"I don't know," she replied. "I just got the weirdest call from Mom, something about an e-mail."

"We got it, too. Both Katie and me. Are you safe?"

"Yes, I'm with Henry. What on earth is going on?"

"The e-mail went to all our clients. Security has disabled your phone and computer."

"Why?"

"This e-mail is nasty, Ellie. I guess it could be your photo cropped over some girl's body. Asking for...

partners. Your cell number's listed. Tell me you didn't do this."

How could you even think? Her lunch was coming up. The world spun rapidly. Ellie dropped the cell phone and shoved the door open. The bitter taste of vomit gagged her.

In a flash Henry set the brake and killed the engine. Then he raced around the car to hover next to her, pulling her hair back. "I'm here, Ellie. Always will be."

***

Henry pulled up a block away from the Optimum and parked. The fog hung in low clumps, just above the lampposts. Ellie stared ahead, without seeing. Henry touched her hand.

"What?" She jumped in her seat, obviously rattled by all that she'd learned and probably terrified by what would come next.

Fear. She'd been near catatonic since her conversation with Kaitlin. Feelings of bitterness, despair, and hopelessness washed over her, each in turn.

"We're here," Henry said. "The hotel. Would you rather I go in and pick up your computer?"

Ellie's breath came in rough clusters. "I don't think I can ever step foot in there again. Would you mind?"

Henry touched her face. She trembled and pulled away. "Of course not," he answered. "I'll go."

As he walked to the Optimum, he saw them. Scores of handbills on almost every public surface. His mouth dropped open. The image was one of the most despicable he'd ever seen, but the worst thing was... Ellie's face had been cropped onto it. *Damn you, Heidi. I know you did this.* He headed inside the hotel.

Horror choked him, Ellie's! Henry grabbed her belongings from Security as quickly as possible and bolted back outside. Ellie was on her knees a half-block away, clutching one of the posters she must've pulled off the notice board. Her head was buried in her hands. Her whole body convulsed with sobs.

"Ignore that filth," he said, trying to lift her up. "That's not you."

Ellie suddenly collapsed into a fetal position. Devastation. Shame. She didn't respond to anything Henry did. Ultimately he scooped her in his arms and carried her away from that hellish place.

***

Ellie's world was crumbling. *Why me?* The character assassination was complete. She wanted to find a tall cliff and jump off. Being recalled to Chicago, like a naughty child had been bad enough, but...

Ellie stuffed her clothes in the suitcase. Her tears wouldn't stay inside. *Losing you is more than I can take.*

Henry cleared his throat. He stood in the doorway. "I can help," he said.

Ellie quickly shook her head before she lost her nerve. "I just need a little alone time, please."

"I see," Henry mumbled half-heartedly. "I'll be in the next room. I love you, Ellie."

She held it together until he disappeared down the hall, then Ellie collapsed on the bed. *You'll forget me in time. But I'll never forget you.*

Ellie cried herself to sleep. Bitter nightmares haunted her, accompanied by her mother's taunts, 'filthy little slut... bitch... whore... do you really think he'd still want you?' Her mother appeared before her, laughing maniacally while shaking her by both shoulders.

Ellie bolted awake. Henry.

"Ellie, we've got to head to the airport."

Her breath was rapid and shallow. His green eyes full of compassion. *How will I live without you?*

"I've packed the car," he said. "What else can I do?"

She looked away, not wanting to meet his eyes. *Hardest thing will be to walk away from you.*

The ride to the airport was in total silence. Henry couldn't possibly understand. *It's for your own good.*

He pulled up to the curb and transferred her luggage to a red cap. *You're the best friend I've ever had. I'll miss you so much.*

Henry drove off to park the car and caught up to her just as she'd finished getting her printed boarding pass. He had a duffel bag in one hand and walked with her all the way to the Security line.

Ellie's heart was breaking. Time to say goodbye. *Who'd want me now?*

She knew her eyes were moist. She turned to him. "Knowing you has been the best blessing of my life. I'll always love you and..."

Henry engulfed her in his arms. "Stop. You're being silly. I won't let you."

"Let me what?"

"Leave me," he replied firmly. "Not ever. I love you too much. If you send me away I'll just follow. 'Til the end of time."

Ellie choked on her words. "Don't make this harder than..."

He held her cheeks and looked deeply into her eyes. "I'm coming with you," he said. "I told you that I love you, forever." With one hand he reached into a coat pocket and pulled out his phone to show her the electronic boarding pass. He'd bought a last-minute ticket on her flight! "As long as I have breath in my body," he whispered, "you'll never be alone."

***

Henry flagged down a cab outside the Chicago airport. Despite Ellie's protestations, he'd accompanied her. She didn't tell him in words, but he knew she was comforted by his presence. They left their bags at the guard station in the lobby. He felt it. Fear of the unknown.

The elevator doors opened. Kaitlin was waiting right outside them in the reception lobby. She frowned when she saw Henry.

Her voice was bland. "You can't stay here, Henry. You'll have to leave."

"I understand," he said. He could feel the panic coming off Ellie in waves. He turned to her and asked, "Where should I meet you later?"

Before Ellie could answer, Kaitlin muttered, "You'll stay with us." Kaitlin jotted down the address on the back of a business card she snatched from the receptionist's desk. "Don't leave. You might have to take a cab, but let me see if I can make arrangements first. The two of us will see you there tonight."

Ellie reached for Henry, but Kaitlin added, "Not here, Ellie. Just say goodbye."

Ellie's eyes started to tear. Henry held his fist to his chest and said, "Courage, my love. Everything will be all right, I promise. I love you. I'll be waiting."

Ellie followed Kaitlin through the office doors. Henry sat in the lobby, but his heart and mind were inside with the girl with the angel's face, his Ellie. He asked God to give her strength.

Forty minutes later, a middle-aged lady with graying curly hair came out and turned to him.

"Are you Henry Campbell?" Her tone was anything but friendly.

He stood and bowed. "I am." He extended his hand. She shook it firmly, clearly assessing everything from his height and eye color to the depths of his soul. He felt naked before her.

"I'm Martina Davis, Eleanor's aunt. I have a court date in ninety minutes so let's move."

She said nothing when he retrieved Ellie's luggage and his duffel. Her BMW SUV slipped swiftly into traffic.

"I've heard about you, Mr. Campbell," she said, "but had no idea you were coming. Judging by my conversation with Kaitlin, she wasn't aware, either. Why are you here?"

"Ellie, I mean... Eleanor, needed someone to comfort her. She's distraught."

"I would be, too, after what happened." She glanced at him briefly. "I also received that disgusting e-mail. That wasn't our Eleanor."

"We saw the postings near the hotel. Quite appalling. I wish Ellie never had to lay eyes on that."

"Does she know who did this?"

"No, but I do. I'm sure it was my ex-girlfriend, Heidi Fries. She wasn't happy when I left her for Ellie. She designs websites and has those kind of skills."

Martina turned onto a highway. "The perfect suspect. Motive. Resources." She reached into the back seat and handed him a pad. "Write down her contact information."

"Why?"

"I want to talk to her," she said insistently.

"Heidi can be quite headstrong. I doubt she'll talk to you."

"Let me tell you something," Martina seethed. "When I'm done with her, she'll wish she was never born."

The look in her eyes concerned Henry.

The woman spared a cursory glance at him. "I'm guessing Eleanor didn't tell you, but I'm an attorney, and a damned good one. You may call me Aunt Martina."

"A-a-aunt?"

Martina rolled her eyes. "P-leeease. Kaitlin told me all about you and Ellie. I don't need a judge and jury to tell me how much you love her."

Auntie grilled him during the rest of the drive. Henry wiped his brow when they finally pulled into the driveway of a large house.

Much to his surprise, Martina grabbed him in a tight hug. "Thank you, Henry. For loving Ellie." She kissed his forehead. "The judge won't wait for me. See you later."

Henry unloaded the bags and watched her pull away. *My heart's with you, Ellie.*

"Ahem."

He turned. Before him stood an elderly couple. Their hair was gray, but the smiles they sported were vibrant. The woman carried her beauty like a halo. She gripped his hands.

"So tall. So handsome. Just like Ellie said. Welcome to our home, Henry. I'm Nora and this is my groom, Stan. Ellie's our favorite granddaughter."

Stan's grip almost brought him to his knees. "So proud to have a Royal Marine stay with us. Former tanker, myself. Nora's cooking bangers and mash and I've got ale on ice. Come inside. Our home is yours."

The afternoon passed quickly. Ellie had certainly talked about her grandparents before, but in no way did she do them justice. So wonderful, so kind. *Just like my Ellie.*

Henry eventually sauntered to the swing on the porch. The heat of the autumn afternoon was warmer than he was accustomed to. The sun was poised in cloudless blue skies. But the beauty of the day was lost on him. *Ellie.* Her feelings were screaming inside him even at this distance. Pain. Anger. Humiliation. Despair. *Comfort her, Lord.* He fell asleep dreaming of Ellie.

Chapter 21

Kaitlin escorted Ellie to the conference room. Kaitlin closed the door and within seconds her cold exterior melted and she turned to hug Ellie. "I'm s-so sorry," she quavered.

Ellie clung to her aunt with sudden relief. "Why would anyone do this?" she asked, then abruptly pulled away. "You don't still think I did this?"

Kaitlin wiped Ellie's eyes. "The thought never crossed my mind. I know you too well."

Ellie fought back a sob. "Did I tell you Mom called me? She's convinced I did this. She called me a, a... I can't even say it. Why does she hate me so much?"

"We'll talk about your mom's issues later. Let's focus on work," Kaitlin said. "This meeting won't be pleasant. John Stange is on sabbatical and Bob Hanes refers to himself as the 'new sheriff in town'. It's been hell here all morning. The man only cares about the company's image. He won't give a crap about what you've been through."

Ellie held her chin high. "I'll quit. That'll solve everything."

Kaitlin gripped her arms tightly. "The hell you will. You did nothing wrong."

"Katie's right," Jeremy chimed in. Ellie hadn't noticed him seated on the couch in the room. "You're the victim, not the villain," he added. Jeremy reached for her.

Just at that moment the door swung open wide. "Isn't this precious?" snorted a man's voice. "What number will our Security Director be on your list, Miss Lucia?"

All three of them turned to stare.

"You're disgusting, Bob Hanes," Kaitlin growled.

Hanes smiled while Ellie could see Jeremy's hands curl into fists. He took a step towards Hanes.

Another woman stepped up behind the new man. Deb Hartwell, Human Resources Manager. "That was uncalled for," she chastised and pushed her way into the office. Taking note of everyone's postures, she added, "Stand down, Jeremy. He's just baiting you." Then she turned back to Hanes. "And you, watch your inferences. Is that clear, Mr. Hanes?"

"Of course, Ms. Hartwell. I'd never tarnish the excellent reputation of this fine establishment. Let's get this over with."

Jeremy and Kaitlin bracketed Ellie at one end of the table. Hanes sat at the other and Deb Hartwell sat in the middle. Hanes pulled a cigarette from a pack with his lips.

Jeremy snarled, "We have a strict no smoking policy here. I'd like to remind you that..."

"You aren't the fire marshal in this building," Hanes fumed. "Such dedication. I wish you had this type of drive for your assigned job. If you did, then maybe your niece..." Hanes paused, watching the rising anger in Jeremy's face. "Didn't think anyone knew about your little family secret? Did you think I just fell off the turnip truck?"

Ellie wanted to crawl out under the door.

Hanes stared at Ellie. "Answer a question, Miss Lucia. Did you send out that e-mail?"

Ellie struggled to keep it together. "No sir, I didn't."

"Was that pornographic website yours or did you appear on it in any way, shape or form?"

Jeremy stood. "The photo on the e-mail was clearly photoshopped..."

"I'm not talking to you, Roberts." Hanes again turned to Ellie. "You mean to tell me none of those images were you?"

This was the worst day in Ellie's life. She was about done. "No, sir. I haven't actually seen the website, but I can tell you, I would never do anything like that."

"You'd swear on a stack of Bibles you had absolutely nothing to do with this?"

She nodded. "That's correct."

Hanes grunted and shifted some papers in front of him. "I should still fire you for damaging our reputation, but Human Resources won't allow it. You deserve to be punished, but since I can't do that, you'll have to help us save face." Hanes turned to Kaitlin and asked, "What's the recovery plan? I assume you *have* a recovery plan, Ms. Roberts?"

Kaitlin's eyes were icy beams. "Of course, Mr. Hanes. I hope you don't think I just fell off the turnip truck."

***

Henry checked his watch. Eight-thirty. He'd been praying for Ellie all day. Devastation. Sadness. Headlights suddenly swept across the lawn.

In the glow of the exterior lights, he could see the anger and frustration in their eyes. Both women had been crying. He opened the back door and took Ellie's arm and guided her inside.

Nora appeared. "Homemade chicken noodle soup's in the crock pot. Anyone like me to dip them some?"

Kaitlin hugged her mother tightly. "Love some. Can you make me a to-go cup?"

"But you just got home," Nora sighed.

Anguish. Sorrow. Ellie's hands trembled. "Katie, I'm sorry. I didn't mean for you to take my place in all this."

Kaitlin's anger came out. "Quit apologizing. It's not your fault. Hanes is a jerk for making me leave tonight. Well, he's a jerk anyway, but..."

"Just quit," Jeremy interrupted her. "We'll be fine. Don't..."

"No. I worked too hard to give up my career because of that asshole."

Henry was confused. "Wait... Are you and Ellie going to London?" He turned to Ellie. "Are you leaving tonight?"

Ellie burst into tears and ran out the front door. She slammed it behind her.

Kaitlin touched his arm. "I'm going alone. I need to finish Ellie's London assignment. Hanes has demoted me and reassigned Ellie. Just let her calm down before you try to comfort her. She's pretty upset."

Bitterness. Sorrow. Henry went to the kitchen and dipped a bowl of chicken soup. He placed three crackers in it, as she liked. He poured a glass of tea, sweetening it how Ellie preferred, and placed it on a tray along with the mums he'd picked for her.

He found Ellie on the front porch seated on the swing. Headlights from a passing car revealed the moistness on her cheeks. He placed the tray on a small table next to the swing and kissed and held her hand.

Ellie stared at the road. Suddenly she broke down. Henry drew her closer and kissed her hair. "Everything will be all right," he whispered. "I brought you something warm to eat."

"I'm not hungry," Ellie sniffled.

He kissed her brow. "Eleanor Faye Lucia, listen to me. No one knows you like I do. Do you believe I can feel what you feel?"

He heard Ellie's long slow inhale and exhale before she answered, "With all my heart."

"I know exactly what you're feeling. Should I tell you?"

She turned to look at him. "Okay. I'd love that."

Henry placed fingertips to his head at his temples, as if to read her thoughts. "I feel it... coming in loud and clear. You're feeling... here it comes... you're feeling... *hungry*. And badly in need of a kiss by someone who loves you more than life itself." He kissed her. Her lips were salty.

Ellie squeezed him tightly. Henry felt it. Panic. Fear. Loss.

"What's wrong?" he asked.

"Hanes has relocated me to Seattle." She pulled back and searched his eyes. "That's even further away from you. What happens if we... if w-we come apart? If you stop loving me... I couldn't take that. Your love is the only thing that got me through today."

"Ellie, I've promised you..."

Her eyes pleaded with him. "I'll quit!" she exclaimed. "I'll come back to London with you, okay? We'll get married."

Such pain. How can I comfort you?

Her eyes were shiny, again. "I'm so scared," she blubbered. "I'm scared you'll go and never come back."

"Never. We're one, inseparable. Only death can keep my love from you. I think we should get married, although I'd rather wait and marry in front of our families. But if you can't wait any longer, I'm yours. Let's get married tonight."

Ellie's mouth dropped open. "Are you serious?"

"Yes. I love you. I'll do whatever you want."

Her lips joined his, sending a twinge of pleasure through his body. Her nose was wet from crying, but Henry didn't care. Contentment. Love. Peace... Happiness.

Chapter 22

llie plopped into the soft easy chair in her extended stay room. Previous renters must have had a dog. She was constantly finding pet hair on her clothes. From a distance of six thousand miles away, she could still feel it. Love. Longing. Wanting her. *I should have run away with you that night.*

She grabbed her laptop and opened her mail box. Forty e-mails, mostly from Henry, but Sophie and Margaret also kept in touch daily. *Closer than family.* On the lonely weekends, the girls video chatted for hours while Henry skyped her a couple of times a day. She knew he sacrificed sleep to talk with her.

Another e-mail pinged. *What the...?* From her new boss. It read: "Ellie, It's been a pleasure working with you. Clean out your desk tomorrow and report to the CEO's office at 8:00 A.M. Monday. Best wishes in all you do."

Fear gripped her like a vise. "I didn't do anything wrong. What's going on?"

Ellie quickly called Kaitlin, who was now back in Chicago. No answer. She got Jeremy's voicemail. Her hands were shaking. She almost jumped from the chair when her phone rang. Henry.

"Hello?" she snapped.

"Ellie, I just got the weirdest feeling something happened. Is everything okay?"

"No, I just got this cryptic e-mail from my boss." For the next half hour, she poured out her heart and feelings.

"Everything will be fine," Henry consoled.

"What if it isn't?"

"It's only a job. We'll get through it. Remember, I'll be there Wednesday night. I'll just meet you in Chicago instead of Seattle."

In her worries, she'd forgotten Henry would be spending the Thanksgiving holidays with her. It would be the last time she'd see him before he finished his assignment in April. He wouldn't be able to come stateside at Christmas because it was high tourist season, but Margaret had promised to visit her then.

"Our love's what's important. Can't wait to see you. And remember, we decided to get married on April 17th, your birthday. I'll never leave your side again," he promised.

His strength. His love. "You're already here with me, now. I can feel it."

"As I feel you. We're one. On your best and your worst days, I'll always be with you."

***

Ellie dreaded the thought of facing Bob Hanes again. She returned to Chicago on Saturday morning after a redeye flight. Kaitlin and Jeremy were in exceptionally good moods, but refused to discuss work at all. The only thought that bolstered her courage was that in just four days, she and Henry would be together again.

Monday morning arrived earlier than she hoped. Ellie drove into the city by herself. Jeremy and Kaitlin had left earlier. When she stepped off the elevator, a uniformed security officer was waiting.

Ellie's heart leapt into her throat.

The officer led her to Hanes' office and said, "Have a seat."

Seconds later, Jeremy and Kaitlin walked in.

Jeremy's smile was wide. "Morning, Ellie. I brought you a cup of coffee."

Kaitlin's laugh thoroughly confused her, but they sat on either side of her, quietly drinking their coffee.

"Am I in trouble?"

Kaitlin snickered. "Why would you think that?"

"The last time I was in here was the day after... well, let's just say I don't have a good feeling about this meeting."

Kaitlin ignored her, resting her feet on the coffee table. "I wonder what time old fuddy-duddy will show up."

A gruff voice growled from the doorway. "Get your filthy feet off my furniture, Ms. Roberts, or else."

The big black chair behind the desk spun around. John Stange! "Or what, Hanes?" he quipped. "By the way, that's my coffee table, not yours."

Hanes recoiled in the doorway. "Who the hell are you?"

"John Stange, CEO. Sit down. I have something for each of you."

First he turned to Ellie. "Miss Lucia, so good to see you again. On behalf of GDC, I apologize for the horrible way you were treated. I have read the investigation. Anyone with even a fifth grade education could see this wasn't your fault. You should have received help instead of being exiled." Stange glared at Hanes.

Hanes studied his fingernails.

Stange shook his head and continued, "Ellie, I can't change what happened, but there's something I can do. Effective immediately, you've been reinstated to Operations, but now, you're in training for a management position, anywhere you want. The successful opening of the Optimum was due in large part to you. You've a bright future ahead of you. Congratulations." Stange stood and handed her an envelope. "The Board expresses their gratitude for your service. Someone said marriage might be in your future. I suspect this'll help."

Ellie gasped when she opened it. Her words were soft. "This is very generous."

"You earned it." Stange shook her hand.

Ellie sniffed. "Thank you, Mr. Stange, for everything."

Stange nodded and smiled. He turned to Kaitlin. "You shouldn't have been demoted or sent to England. I'm just relieved you didn't quit. Instead you sacrificed for this company, leaving your children for several weeks, with no notice. I wish others were half as dedicated as you."

Hanes yawned and looked out the window.

Stange handed Kaitlin an envelope. "This is a gift, of gratitude. You've been reinstated as Ops Manager, with apologies from the Board."

Kaitlin glanced inside and smiled. "Thanks, John."

"Enjoy the time off, as well as returning to the position you worked so hard to get."

Stange patted Jeremy on the shoulder. "You also sacrificed when Kaitlin went to London. You deserve time off, too. So go somewhere special, on us. Hang around. Got something else for you, too."

Deb Hartwell walked in and handed an envelope to Stange.

Stange turned to Hanes. "You were hired to be the acting CEO in my absence, correct?"

Hanes laughed. "Save the theatrics. My job's finished. Guess I'll head back to New Jersey. You can deposit my bonus in my account."

Stange rubbed his chin. "About that. That bonus was only guaranteed, *provided* you acted in the company's best interests. Everyone agrees you failed."

"What?"

Stange faced him. "Any manager worth his salt knows you don't treat people like you did. Especially not *my* people. The Board has decided to remove you. Unanimous vote. No bonus and... you're fired. Leave."

Hanes grabbed Stange's collar, until Jeremy bent Hanes' arm into an unnatural position. Hanes howled in pain.

Stange laughed. "Mind taking out the trash?"

"It'd be my honor," Jeremy replied.

Hanes cursed. "My attorney will be in touch. You won't get away with this."

Stange tucked an envelope into Hanes' shirt pocket. "We just did, Hanes. Get this scum away from me."

"With pleasure." Jeremy dragged Hanes towards the elevator.

Stange laughed. "It's almost Thanksgiving. We all have much to be thankful for. Let's start the holiday early, say in about two minutes? That's a direct order from the real CEO."

Chapter 23

*H*enry's legs were cramped after the long flight from London. He felt Ellie. Anticipation. Wonder. Love. London had been so lonely after Ellie left. Sophie and Ben were married the week after the tower-top proposal and moved to the States, to a place called Paradise in a province called Pennsylvania. *When Ellie's my wife, I'll be in paradise, too.*

As soon as he cleared the airport checkpoint, he heard Ellie's squeal. Henry dropped the bags. Ellie leapt into his arms and they blended together for several minutes. Her scent was heavenly, her taste divine. "Missed you so much. Can't wait until I never have to leave your side again."

Ellie's eyes sparkled. "So good to hold you. I love you."

Henry retrieved his luggage and they walked to her truck. Inside the pickup, she reached for him again. Her hair was askew and his face was covered in red lipstick when they eventually came up for air. But something was amiss. He felt happiness, but also fear, immense fear.

"What's wrong?"

"Oh," she giggled, "I forgot you can feel me. My parents are in town for the weekend. I'm just scared what they'll say when they meet you."

"Would you prefer I didn't come to the house?"

"No. I love you. You're my life, my everything. But... for years now, nothing I did was good enough for them. They didn't like Ben. Hated Steve. I'm afraid they won't be nice to you. We haven't spoken since that day... well, I tried calling and texting, but neither one of them will answer. They hate me and I don't know why."

He brushed the hair from her eyes. "Tell me what to do."

"I don't know. I'm afraid they'll be nasty and you'll leave."

Never. He held her face. "Brand this on your heart. I'll never leave. I love you, Ellie. Until eternity passes away. Should I smother them with kindness?"

She shook her head. "If you were with anyone else besides me, they'd bend over backwards to be kind. But you're with me, so this will go badly."

He kissed her lips. "I'll tell them how much I love you. Let them know I am going to marry you. Nothing will change that. The world may be against us, but we have each other. That's all we need."

They arrived at a house Henry had never seen. Before they went in, they prayed.

Martina opened the door. "Look who's here." She hugged them both and kissed his cheek. Martina turned to call the rest of the family.

Astonishment. "What is it, Ellie?"

Ellie giggled. "Why, Henry Campbell! I never saw my aunt kiss anyone before, except her hubby and kids. Look at you go, Mr. Irresistible."

Kaitlin and Jeremy appeared, followed by the rest of Ellie's family. Jeremy shook his hand, but Kaitlin kissed Henry on both cheeks. Nora also kissed the side of his face, causing Ellie to snicker.

Henry was so happy for her. Finally he felt the joy in her soul. A wide smile covered her face. It was like a beautiful day in Kensington Park. But that quickly faded. Panic. Dread. She stared past him. Henry turned to follow her gaze.

A dark-haired man and an attractive middle-aged woman stood at the end of the hall.

The man nodded at Ellie. "Been a long time. You look good."

Ellie smiled, but Henry knew it was forced. Apprehension. "Good to see you again, Dad. This is my boyfriend, Henry Campbell."

"A pleasure to meet you, Mr. Lucia," Henry said as he offered his hand. The man nodded, but didn't reach out. Henry dropped his hand to his side when the man walked away. The woman paused awkwardly then came over.

Ellie's face showed no emotion. "Hello, Mom. Henry, this is my mother, Cassandra Lucia."

Henry bowed. "A pleasure to meet you, ma'am."

She looked at Henry without saying a word, then turned to Ellie. "Well, well. The prodigal daughter returns. Look everyone, it's the American Slut back from her whirlwind tour of London. Is he a repeat sex partner or someone you just met outside? Have you achieved your goal of five hundred men yet?"

Henry's face heated. He held his tongue and glanced at Ellie. Devastation. Tears tracked down her cheeks.

"Good to see you too, Mom."

What a witch! How could anyone treat Ellie that way? *Her own mother?* Henry's blood boiled. It hurt Henry, but he could feel Ellie's deep pain.

Before Henry could respond, Cassandra did. Her eyes were wild. "I can't say the same. How dare you ruin our family's name with your little porn stunts? Allowing people to photograph and video you, then posting them on the web. Sending out e-mails asking for more partners? You're the world's biggest slut and you'll rot in

Hell. Whore! I hate you. I wish you were never born. I regret every breath you ever drew."

She raised her arm to strike Ellie, but Henry jumped between them.

"Get away from her!" He shoved Cassandra back violently. *No one will touch Ellie. I'll kill anyone who tries.*

Martina ran over, separating Henry and Cassandra. "Stop it! Cassie, there are children in this house. You will refrain from future vulgar outbursts." Then Martina turned to Henry and said, "Stand down. Now."

Cassandra screamed, "I won't stop until that bitch gets out of my life for good. Kick her out, Tina. There are decent people in this house. I never want to see that girl's ugly, acne-pocked face again."

Martina's voice quivered. "Stop it, Cassie. Ellie's always welcome here, but if you don't control yourself, I'll kick you out. Understand?"

Ellie was gasping for air. "Not necessary, Aunt Tina. You win, Mother. You'll never have to see my ugly, scarred face again, any of you!" She grabbed Henry's hand and pulled him back toward the front door. "I want to leave. Come with me, please?"

Henry was seething. "Yes. Let's go."

Kaitlin pulled Ellie from Henry's grasp and hugged her close. "Please don't go."

Ellie was struggling. Complete ruination of her soul. "I'm not wanted here," she said. Ellie turned to her family. "I'm sorry you all think I trashed our name. But I didn't do anything. If you knew the first thing about me, you'd know it's not true."

Ellie pushed Kaitlin away forcefully, then ran out the door. Henry grabbed their coats, following hotly in pursuit.

***

Henry had to run to catch up. Ellie stumbled and cried uncontrollably. Disbelief. Henry finally was able to reach an arm around her shoulder and pull her close. "I'm so sorry. What can I do?"

Ellie handed her truck keys to him. "Just drive, Henry. Take me away from this horrid place."

Henry helped her into the truck.

Jeremy suddenly banged on Ellie's window and shouted, "Please don't leave!"

Henry shifted into gear and pulled onto the street, tugging Ellie close so she could cry on his shoulder. After about twenty minutes, they finally arrived at Kaitlin and Jeremy's home.

Ellie led him to her room. Her tears were subsiding. "Henry, call Sophie. She had wanted us to visit with them this weekend. Suddenly I don't want to stay in Chicago anymore, not with my parents here. Let's go visit Sophie and Ben."

"Calm down."

Anger! Before Henry knew what was coming, Ellie slapped him, hard.

"Are you nuts?" she yelled. "The worst day of my life and you want me to calm down? You just stay here. I'm going to Pennsylvania. I thought you loved me. Go to Hell, you Scottish bastard. I don't care what you do, just get away from me."

Henry grabbed her, drawing her close. She struggled, kicked, pinched and drilled her high heel repeatedly into his instep, ranting and raving as he held her close. It hurt like hell, but not even God Himself could make him let go.

When she started to quiet down, he kissed her hair. "Ellie. I'm sorry. I didn't mean to offend you. I apologize. Where you go, I do, too. We'll go to Pennsylvania together. I love you. I'm here. Always will be." She stopped struggling and clung tightly to him, still crying intensely.

"Why do my parents hate me? Why'd Mom have to do that, in front of everyone? I'll never be able to face any of them again, ever."

A door slammed downstairs.

"I never imagined a mother could be so cruel to her child," Henry commiserated. "Don't know what to say but this... I'll always love you, no matter what. On your best days or worst days, I'll always be yours and yours alone."

She wiped her cheeks. "Sorry to be stuck with me?"

Low self-esteem. He touched her face to look into her eyes. "I've never considered it *being stuck* with you. Knowing you is an honor. Being with you, pure joy. Your love's the greatest blessing of my life. You're perfect, in every way, Ellie. Understand what I mean when I tell you I love you. It means I want to spend every second of my life with you. I'd give you the shirt off my back in a storm to keep you warm. My last bite of food if you were hungry. Lay down my life if it meant saving yours. I love you, forever."

Her tears started again. No sorrow now. Only love. Appreciation. She kissed him. "I couldn't make it through this life without you. Sorry I said those things to you."

"I was wrong. Ellie. Forgive me."

A knock sounded on the door. Kaitlin's voice called, "Ellie? May I come in?"

Ellie opened the door. It was apparent that Kaitlin had also been crying. She pulled Ellie into a tight embrace and the two women clung to each other. "I'm sorry for what happened," she said. "It was completely undeserved. You're loved and wanted in this family."

Ellie rubbed her eyes. "Not everyone feels like you do. My mother ran me into the ground. My father didn't even say a word. And did you see the look on the twins' faces? Smirks. Mom never wants to see me again? She's got it. I'm done, I have no family."

Henry saw the tears in Kaitlin's eyes.

"That's not true," Kaitlin replied. "I love you. Jeremy loves you. Everyone loves you more than you'll ever know. We'll always be your family, but we need to talk about your mom. She needs to explain why she acted that way. Can she come over tomorrow?"

Ellie shook her head. "I have no mother anymore. I've been the red-headed bastard stepchild in this family for too long. I'm done." She opened her hand. Henry quickly took it. "This is Henry. He's my family now."

Kaitlin grabbed her shoulders. "Your mom needs to explain. We all need to get past this. Let her come over."

Ellie shrugged her shoulders. Confidence. Resolve. "She can come over whenever she wants. But we won't be here."

"Where are you going? Ellie, be reasonable."

Ellie's eyes were ablaze. "Be reasonable? She accused me of being the biggest whore in the world in front of everyone I care about and you tell me to be reasonable? What is wrong with you?"

"It's Thanksgiving. Please don't harbor anger and resentment. Don't stoop to your mother's level. Hear her out. I think you'll want to forgive her. I'll be there if it'll help."

"Aunt Katie, I'm an orphan now. We're flying to Pennsylvania to visit Ben and Sophie. I'll never celebrate Thanksgiving with my old family, ever."

Kaitlin turned to Henry. "Please talk some sense into her."

Henry shook his head. "Kaitlin, you've been so nice to me. But don't ask me to come between you and Ellie. I love her and will always do what she wants. I'm truly sorry about that."

Kaitlin kissed Ellie's cheek and said, "You're making a very big mistake. I beg you, don't do this."

Ellie's tears were gone now. Poise. Self-assuredness. "I'm doing this. I want to be with people who love me, unconditionally."

Chapter 24

Ellie started to wake. It'd been a late night. They'd caught a direct flight into Philadelphia, disembarking at five minutes before midnight.

Her mind drifted back to last evening. Sophie and Ben were waiting and grabbed Ellie in a tight embrace. Ellie saw Sophie pull Henry into the group hug. The four stayed up until early morning talking and getting caught up on life. *Exactly what I needed.*

"I told my Aunt Kaitlin that Henry's my only family now."

Sophie embraced her. "So not true. You're my sister, by choice, and damned proud to say it."

Lying in bed, Ellie thanked God for close friends, and Henry. Her eyes lazily focused on the slow rotation of the ceiling fan. Henry shifted position. Ellie rolled and looked toward him. His intense green eyes smiled at her. *My heart's yours, always.* Henry softly kissed her lips, then pulled away.

"My love, may I ask a question?"

It was pure bliss to be in his arms. "Ask me anything you desire and the answer will be yes."

Henry blushed. "We're waiting, remember?"

"Darn. What'd you want to ask?"

His eyes were filled with merriment. "How can it be that you slept all night, yet your lips taste like honey? This isn't natural. Not that I've lots of experience kissing girls in bed first thing in the morning, but seriously, how can your kisses be so sweet every time our lips meet?"

Waited my whole life for you. That earned him another deep kiss. She knew her dimples appeared.

"Ellie, may I call you honey, as a pet name?"

"I'd love that, on one condition."

"Name it."

"When we get married, wake me every morning, just like this."

"Deal. Glad you brought up our wedding. Where do you want to get married?"

Her throat closed. Even after last night... "Do you know how much I love you?"

Playfulness. "Just a little bit less than I love you!"

Laughter. "Impossible! I love you more!"

"No, honey. I love you most."

She traced his lips with her finger. "Let's call a truce. We love each other the exact same amount, okay?"

The taste of his lips was driving her wild. "Agreed, honey."

Such wonderful feelings of love. He touched her cheek gently. "You're so beautiful, but it isn't your beauty I fell in love with. It's what's inside of you that I love so much. Just because you're you."

That earned him another very wet kiss. "I love you, Henry."

After showers, they sauntered downstairs. Sophie was preparing a dish for Thanksgiving. Sophie smiled. "Benjy, look who finally woke up. Morning, love birds."

Ben turned, coffee in hand. "You two sleep well? Want coffee or tea?"

At peace. Ellie returned the smile. "Yes, we did and yes, we would, please. I crave coffee, but Henry wants tea, both extra strong." Ellie stopped when she noticed the strange look on Sophie's face.

Sophie walked around the counter and took Ellie's hands. "You've a glow about you this morning. So relaxed." She turned to Henry, studying his face. "Henry, oh my. Benjy. Look at this. I think our guests have been naughty this morning. No doubt, they've that after love-making glow. That bed is quite comfortable, isn't it?"

Embarrassment. Henry blushed and Ellie laughed. "Sophie! A little, but not completely naughty, not yet. We're waiting for the wedding, but we did..." Henry squeezed her hand. Terror. Ellie giggled.

"Ellie! Don't tell them what we did."

She winked at him. "Henry, get used to it. Sophie and I share everything. We're sisters. Isn't that right, Soph?"

Sophie laughed at Henry. "Don't be a boor. We're sisters and we share everything. We're all adults. Maybe this will make you feel better. You two weren't the only ones who were naughty this morning, were they, Benjy?"

Henry placed his hands over his ears. "I don't want to hear any more. Tell me all of America isn't like this, please?"

Ben clapped him on the back. "No, just this part of Pennsylvania. Our home is in two townships. Your bedroom is in Paradise Township while ours is in Intercourse."

Disbelief. Henry's mouth dropped open. "Intercourse? Dear Lord."

"Down the road is Virginville." He pointed northwest. "Over there's Bird in Hand and who can forget Blue Ball? Shall I go on?"

Ellie laughed so hard she thought she'd pee herself! "This is Pennsylvania Dutch country and some towns have unusual names." Ellie kissed him. "I love teasing you."

The teasing continued through breakfast. Henry's ears turned red in embarrassment. Afterwards, Ben and Sophie gave them a tour.

Sophie gave the narrative like the seasoned guide that she was. She pointed to a large stone barn just outside. "Here's where we'll raise cows. Next year, we'll build a chicken coop."

They strolled around the property. Next to their barn, the remains of an old, very large stone house stood, overgrown with weeds.

Ben said, "That was my great grandparents' home. Mom inherited the estate when her mother passed away. She subdivided the farm into four lots. Ours is one lot. That place," he pointed to the old house, "is the second lot, about ten acres. There's seven acres down the road and the main farm, three hundred acres. Mom plans to sell them after my sister decides if she's interested."

Something about the farmhouse intrigued Ellie. Her whole body trembled. "Henry, let's take a look." The four walked to where the porch steps once stood. She squeezed his hand. "This place has a lot of charm, and potential. Do you agree?"

Curiosity. Hope. Henry took it all in.

Ellie's excitement was growing in leaps and bounds. "Tell me what you think of it."

Henry smiled at her. *Read my mind.* His eyes closed. "Honey, it's wonderful. I can picture how it used to be."

She spun to face him, searching his eyes. Excitement grew, his face beamed. Henry smiled.

She was happily impatient. "Henry, tell me what you see."

His eyes left the ruins, seeking out hers. "I see us sitting on a swing, watching the sunset together while drinking tea. We snuggle as we discuss our day." He again closed his eyes. "I see us making it our home, Ellie. Planting flowers together, dirt smeared on our noses."

His grip on her hands tightened. "I see us laughing with our children, playing a game of cricket."

Ellie snorted. "Cricket? Henry, you're in America. You mean baseball or softball?"

Henry placed his hands on his hips, clearing his throat. "My Lady, this is my vision." It was all for show. He couldn't keep a straight face.

She kissed his warm hand. "Sorry. Please continue."

He again turned toward the house. Happiness. Dreams coming true. "I feel the warmth of a fire as we gaze at a beautiful tree decorated for the holidays. The snow is piled deep outside, but our love warms the house, no, our *home*. Our children open their gifts while the most beautiful woman in the world and I watch them."

Ben interjected. "Wait a minute. Sophie's the most beautiful woman in the world. We're close friends, but boundaries, please."

Henry's look melted her heart. "Sorry, but she'll never compare to Ellie's beauty."

Sophie slapped his arm. "Ouch, that hurts. Aren't I beautiful?"

"Yes, but Ellie's tops for me."

Ellie sighed as she threaded her arm through his. "I wish it could come true, but we'll be living in Chicago, not Paradise." Her eyes widened. They hadn't discussed it. "Henry..."

Henry embraced her. Comfort. Love. "Wherever you are, that's where home will be for me."

A thought struck her. She turned to Ben. "Wait... You live here. Does that mean you're quitting GDC?"

Ben slowly smiled. "No. When my grandmother passed, I was in Singapore. Hadn't been home in six months. I vowed when I settled down, I'd move back home to be with my family." He pulled Sophie into his arms. "Now that we're married, this is our home. I want our children to know their grandmother and aunt. To grow up here in the country like I did. This is where I'll live and die. This is our home."

"But you work in Chicago. Will you commute from here?"

"I'm tired of travelling for a living. I want to hold my wife in my arms every night. GDC is opening an office forty-five minutes away to support our clients in Philly, New York and New Jersey. I'm the site Security Manager. Maybe you can transfer here."

Ellie turned to look at Henry. Yes. "That's fine with me, if that's what you want." She squealed, hugging him.

Suddenly, Sophie understood what they were talking about. She jumped up and down with joy, happiness visible on her face. "How wonderful! Having my two best friends living close to us, maybe even next to us! I'm so excited."

***

While Sophie and Ellie were dreaming out loud about raising their children together, Henry pulled Ben aside. They walked away from the girls.

"Benjamin, I've got a favor to ask."

"What is it?"

Henry removed a box from his pocket, making sure Ellie didn't see it. He showed the contents to his friend. "I plan on proposing to Ellie this weekend. Is there somewhere special you could take us? Maybe not the Eiffel Tower special, but..."

Ben smiled ear to ear. "I hoped and prayed you two would get married. What do you have in mind? We can be in New York in three hours, the shore in two. Where shall we go?"

"Ellie loves gardens. I know this time of year is kind of drab, but is there any place you could suggest?"

Ben's smile broadened. "I have the perfect place, forty minutes away. We're going to my mother's this afternoon, so today might not work, though."

"Tomorrow?"

Ben shook Henry's hand and said, "Deal. But I have to tell Sophie. She'd kill me if I didn't let her in on it."

"Okay, just don't let her spoil the surprise."

***

Thanksgiving was enjoyable for Ellie, exactly what she needed. Her heart was touched when Sophie introduced her as her chosen sister.

Ben's mother hugged her. "Then you're my daughter, too."

Ben's sister, Tara, kissed her cheek. "Glad to have another sister." That evening, the girls talked about starting a Black Friday shopping tradition, but decided to wait until next year. Ellie thought it was strange. She'd caught the wink Sophie shot at Tara. Ellie suspected something was going on.

The scent of clean cotton and Henry awakened her. After showers, a knock sounded on the door. Henry opened it. Sophie.

"Morning, Henry. Sleep well?"

"Yes, and you?"

"We slept gloriously, Henry, just gloriously." Ellie noted Sophie's eyes were moist, but a larger than life smile graced her face. "Henry, could I borrow your girl for a little bit? I want to do some sister stuff with her. Please go downstairs with Benjy."

Henry quickly said, "See you two downstairs." His heart was full of happiness, anticipation. This was a conspiracy.

Sophie took her hand. Ellie was extremely curious. "You look like you've been crying. What's going on?"

Sophie kissed Ellie's forehead. "Nothing. Life's never been better for me. I just want to take you over to my room, okay?"

"Tell me what's happening."

"Ellie, I love you and am so happy for you. You see, we have so much in common. You aren't the only one whose parents weren't the best. Mine were old by the time I came around. Mum was forty-five when she had me, Pops was fifty-seven. Most of the time they basically ignored me. I dreamed of a close family, but it never happened, until now. Because of you." She hugged Ellie tightly.

Ellie was touched. "Love you too, Soph."

Sophie wiped her eyes. "I'm going to ask you something and on our friendship, I want you to do it, without question. Will you?"

What in the world? "Okay, I'll bite. What do you have in mind?"

"Let's play dress-up today. Get your prettiest thing, then come to my room."

A thought entered her head. *Could it be?* Ellie grabbed the one dress she'd brought, the white one with yellow flowers. Sophie led her down the hall, closed the door and asked her to put on her dress. Then Sophie directed her to a chair.

"I want to repay your kindness. May I do your hair and your makeup?"

Ellie's suspicion grew. "Why?"

"We agreed without question, right?"

Ellie nodded. Over the next twenty minutes, Sophie did Ellie's makeup, then wound her hair into twin braids on top of her head. Ellie looked in the mirror and was astounded. She looked beautiful.

Sophie kissed her hand. "The boys are waiting. Let's have breakfast."

Ellie's curiosity grew when she saw Ben and Henry were dressed in suits. Henry's mouth dropped open. Love. Admiration. His hands were shaking.

"Okay, what's going on?"

Ben answered. "Sophie and I decided today would be a dress-up day."

She caught Henry's look. It hit her. *Today's going to be the day!* Her heart was in her throat, but she kept her thoughts to herself.

After breakfast, Ben drove them to a place called Longwood Gardens. It had been a vast estate owned by the Dupont family. Henry held her hand, but was unusually quiet. Joy filled her. *He's going to propose!*

Henry knew she loved flowers. His anxiety was giving him away. Further proof was when Ben retrieved his digital camera from the trunk.

Henry opened the door for Ellie. She kissed him. "Henry, I want to tell you how much I love you."

"I love you so much, Ellie, at times it almost hurts." Today was one of those days. He kissed her hand. "You look like a princess today, honey. I've never seen anyone as beautiful as you."

His nervousness was there. Ellie shot him a wholesome smile. "I know what's going on." He started to reply, but she kissed him. "Two days ago was a day I want to forget, but today, I'll remember forever. Enjoy today. Calm down. I'll tell you a secret. Okay?"

Henry nodded his head. "I'm a tad bit nervous."

Her dimples came out. "Don't be, you can't lose. I guarantee it. I love you, Henry Campbell. Every single part of me loves you. You're the most wonderful thing to ever happen to me."

Henry smiled. True love.

It started snowing as they entered the gardens. Henry held his jacket over Ellie's head to keep the flakes away. Ben led them to the Conservatory. The trees outside had lost their leaves, but inside was an explosion of green. Poinsettias were stacked in pots on a frame in the shape of a tree. A stream flowed through the glass-enclosed greenhouse. Vibrant flowers shot up amidst the greens. They strolled through the little slice of heaven. At a small overlook, a curved white bench sat facing the stream. Benjy and Sophie continued walking, but Henry and Ellie stopped.

Henry sat next to Ellie, holding her hand. Though the lush vegetation was eye popping, she didn't see it. All she saw was Henry, so handsome, so regal. Ellie's eyes glistened, realizing what was about to happen.

As so many times before, everything else faded. Finally, Henry broke the spell. His voice quivered. "Ellie, you're the love of my life, everything I could ever want, need or desire. I love you, beyond measure." He slowly removed a ring box from his coat pocket.

Ellie looked into the eyes of this man she loved. Their love was so improbable, it must come from God. So much magic between them. This was God's desire for the two of them to be together.

"I love you, Henry, like no man has ever been loved by a woman. You're the answer to my prayers."

Henry bit his lip and lowered himself to one knee. Ellie's eyes began to tear. Henry gently kissed her hand.

"No words I could ever express can tell you how I feel. This story of ours started years before we met. Someone was always there with me. I've no doubt it was you. I loved you since before I knew your name. Never doubted I'd meet you, but never in my wildest dreams did I imagine you'd be so perfect. I've never known anyone more compassionate, loving, or caring than you. That's what I fell in love with."

Ellie could barely believe herself. She'd expected it, but now that it was occurring, it was much more emotional and special than she'd ever dreamed. *This is the most wonderful moment of my life.*

"Ellie, I can't live without you. I need you, every day for the rest of my life. I beg of you," Henry displayed the brilliance of the ring, "Please share this life with me as my wife, my partner, my love, my soul mate. Eleanor Faye Lucia, will you marry me and make me the happiest man in the world?"

Ellie's happiness knew no end. As much as she'd tried not to allow it, her tears came. Her voice trembled. "Henry Thomas Campbell, I waited my entire life for you to come along. I want to spend every second of eternity as your wife. The answer is yes." She grabbed his neck, kissing his lips with an urgency.

He pulled away and softly kissed her hand. Slowly, Henry slipped the ring on her finger. They placed their foreheads together.

Ellie softly prayed, "Dear God, thank You for bringing us together, for making us for each other. We know You meant us to be. We ask You to bless our friendship, our love and our marriage. Thank You, Father."

As Ben promised Henry, Ben and Sophie provided the celebration. Within an hour of Ellie's acceptance, they were bound for New York City. Lunch was a picnic meal on the train. A horse-drawn carriage ride in Central Park, complete with champagne, helped make the afternoon complete. Ben treated them to dinner at the Rainbow Room. The night of romance was complete as Henry held his fiancée in his arms, taking in the Rockefeller tree. As the lights shone brightly, the pair dreamed. No words were spoken or needed. They were one. The day was truly perfect.

Ellie used her time on the way back from New York City to update her Facebook status. She was so happy. She wanted to share it with the world.

***

Kaitlin sat on the couch watching a movie with the extended family. The holiday had been subdued since the blowout Wednesday evening. There was a giant hole in the normally loving family. Sides had been drawn, mostly supporting Ellie, though some supported Cassandra.

The ping sounded on her phone. Kaitlin viewed the screen, then looked up. Everyone else was doing the same. Almost as one, they viewed the pictures Ellie had posted. The first was a photo of Henry and Ellie. Ellie was all smiles as Henry held her closely against a backdrop of orchids. The caption said, 'the future Mr. and Mrs. Henry and Ellie Campbell on the day of their engagement'. A picture of her ring was spectacular. Then Sophie and Ellie were laughing in front of Radio City Music Hall with the caption, 'the two happiest women in the world'. The last was Henry and Ellie sharing a kiss in front of the Rockefeller tree, with the caption, 'true love lasts forever'.

Kaitlin's eyes were scratchy. Almost all of the adults were wiping their cheeks. However, Cassandra started sobbing and ran to the kitchen. Martina followed her. It felt like Ellie was no longer part of the family. They were just spectators now.

Chapter 25

The hustle and bustle of the airport was just background noise. Henry looked into those big brown eyes. *How can I live for the next four months without you?* He could feel her. Sadness. Longing. But above all, love.

"It'll go quick. Besides, Margaret will be here to celebrate Christmas with you."

She was trying so hard to be brave. "Sophie and Margaret promised to help with our wedding preparations." Her cheeks were moist.

"Before I go, I want to give you a present."

"I didn't get you anything."

"Yes, you did. Your love. Now open this."

Ellie wiped her cheeks and tore the wrappings from the box. Her eyes sparkled when she saw it.

"Henry, it's beautiful. But there's two of them."

"Yes. One for you and one for me." He lifted the necklace from the box. "The center is a Celtic knot, signifying our love. It can never be undone."

She kissed his hand. "Is it gold?"

"Yes. Turn it over."

She sobbed as she read the inscription on the back of the silver circle around the gold knot. 'Henry loves Ellie loves Henry.'

"Just like our love. Never ending. I had the inscription put on the back so it always faces your heart. An unbroken bond of love."

He placed it around her neck. Ellie reached up and clasped his into place.

"Forever and always."

"Henry, stay. Let's get married. I don't care about the money. Let's stay together."

"And have you miss three months mentoring in Hawaii, training for your new job? I hear it's paradise."

Her eyes searched his. True love. "Wherever you are, that's where my paradise is."

Henry held her. This was harder than he thought. If she asked one more time, he'd stay.

"Do you promise to video chat with me every day?"

"Only once a day?"

Kissing Ellie goodbye was the hardest thing he'd ever done. Sophie and Ben stood behind her as she waved goodbye. His last sight of her was with her fist to her chest, just like he'd done the night they met. *I'll love you, forever.*

***

Life in London was hell for Henry. His only real friend had been Sophie and now she'd moved to America, with her Benjy. Ellie was half a world away, in Hawaii, mentoring to learn the job she'd do in Pennsylvania. They talked several times every day, but he physically missed her. The sound of her voice. The touch of her hand. The taste of her lips. Her luscious scent. But the thing he missed the most was her twin dimpled smile. He saw them on video, but it wasn't the same.

His office smelled musty, but if he tried hard enough, he could remember the scent of Sophie's perfume. Sophie's contribution to making this place bearable.

Henry thought about Ellie continually. *Thank God we have our feelings.* He could tell when she was happy, when she was sad. Saturdays and Sundays were the best days, spending countless hours on Skype.

He glanced at the calendar. Valentine's Day was coming up. Ellie had teased him, telling him that was the day she'd let him know where they would wed. *Like that would matter. As long as I'm with you.* He counted the days until she would share not only his days, but his name.

***

Ellie walked along the beach, taking in the ocean's smell, soaking in the stars. She needed Henry more than he needed her. Everywhere she went, she saw him. Driving in her car, he was right behind her. Walking on the beach, he frolicked in the waves. She detected his scent in the morning. At night, if she was very quiet, she could hear his voice comfort her. Ellie often cried herself to sleep, hand wrapped tightly on her necklace. She needed Henry now more than food or drink.

Hawaii was lovely, but her loneliness was horrible. Here she was in the most beautiful place in the world, but Henry wasn't there. She wanted nothing more than to share every sight, every memory with him. She texted him dozens of pictures every day. But it wasn't the same as sharing even the most mundane things, in person.

Ellie had arrived in Honolulu during the third week of January. Her mentor, Leleina Robertson was waiting at the airport. It felt like Ellie had known her for years. They headed to Leleina's beach home on the northern shore of Oahu.

"Leleina, I get the distinct feeling I've seen you before."

Leleina laughed. "Call me Lele. You probably have seen me before. Maybe as Miss Hawaii, or possibly from the pineapple commercials they filmed when I was a teenager. I'd take a pineapple ring, bite off the top and hold it in front of my mouth like a smile. The slogan was, 'our fruit is the Pearl of the Pacific, eat our pineapple slices – we grow the pineapple that makes you smile?'"

Ellie's eyes grew wide. "That was you?"

"Yes. My dad brags that my smile sold a billion dollars' worth of pineapples. He tells everyone I'm the one who made the family fortune."

"If your family owns the Pearl of the Pacific fruit business, why do you work for GDC?"

"To get experience. Right out of college, I worked for Southern Pacific for a year, then Starbucks, but I missed Hawaii. GDC manages a lot of businesses on the islands, mostly contracting. Not very glamorous, but it will come in handy when I go to work for Dad."

Ellie's interest was up. "How long until you do that?"

Ellie pondered what it would be like to have Lele's job in Honolulu, but she'd fallen in love with Pennsylvania. She hadn't told Henry, but she'd already purchased the property next to Ben and Sophie. She couldn't wait to tell him that was where they'd be married, in front of the old house they'd make a home. Valentine's Day was when he'd find out. She couldn't wait to see his reaction.

Leleina was an excellent teacher, mentoring Ellie. Her job would be boring after what she did working for Kaitlin. She hadn't told Henry, but her vision matched his when they'd seen the old house. She was willing to sacrifice job satisfaction for happiness in her non work-related life.

Leleina and Ellie became fast friends, exploring the less touristy spots on Oahu. Leleina took her to Maui one weekend, driving down the Road to Hana. The two had become inseparable, spending work and free time together. And that was what caused the problem the day before Valentine's Day.

Leleina's home was on a remote section of the North Shore, totally secluded from the road and neighbors with a private boat dock. On February thirteenth, Ellie and Lele were going to have a cookout on the private beach.

Ellie had just hung up with Henry when the doorbell rang.

"Can you get the door, Ellie?" It was dark outside.

Ellie realized she'd made a terrible mistake when she opened the door. Four men with masks over their heads tried to push past her. Ellie attempted to slam the door shut, but one of them jammed his foot in the door frame.

Ellie screamed a warning, but the men kicked the door open. Two rushed past while two more grabbed her. Ellie delivered a swift kick to the groin on the first attacker. The second one threw her to the floor. The first one ripped her from the floor, her arms behind her. The other masked man pulled something from his pocket, pouring liquid on it. Ellie waited until he came close. When he reached for her, she delivered a vicious head bump, knocking him out.

Lele was screaming for help. The attacker behind her let go and grabbed her hair. Ellie pivoted, delivering three hard punches to his throat. The man crumpled. Ellie kicked his knee, his groin and finally his head. Both attackers were out of action.

Ellie ran to help Lele. The girl was fighting off a man as he tried to clamp a cloth over her face. Ellie looked for a weapon. She grabbed a ceramic lamp, ripping the cord from the socket. Hoisting it high above her head, she slammed it on the crown of Lele's attacker. The lamp shattered and blood gushed from his head. Ellie grabbed Lele's hand, yanking her to her feet, but before she could do anything, the fourth assailant seized Ellie by her left arm. He swung her around and crashed her head into the wall.

Ellie tried to settle herself, but saw stars. The man backhanded Lele, dropping her to the floor. Ellie was ready when he turned his attention to her. She tried a roundhouse kick, but he stepped aside. Too big and fast. Before she could recover, he gripped the back of her neck and slammed her head against a plate glass mirror. The glass shattered, driving slivers into her forehead. She tried to put her hands up to keep him from doing it again, but he slammed her into the mirror repeatedly until she saw no more.

***

Henry was at a stoplight when his heart filled with terror and fear. *Ellie!* He pulled out his mobile, punching her number. There was no answer. He tried again, but it went straight to voicemail. Henry tried texting Ellie. No reply. Something was horribly wrong. Henry called off work and tried to reach her time and again. Nothing. *Please, let her answer.*

When it would have been morning in Hawaii, he couldn't take it anymore. Henry called Sophie, her voice happy as she answered. "Miller residence."

"Sophie, it's Henry. Did you hear from Ellie today?"

"No, I haven't. We were supposed to Skype earlier, but she wasn't online. Is something wrong?"

He was frantic. "I don't know. This morning, I got the feeling something was horribly wrong. I tried calling and texting, but she didn't answer. Something bad happened, I know it."

Her voice was shaky, no longer happy. "I'll call Ben and see if she checked in with him or Jeremy at the Tower."

"I tried her office," Henry said, "but the night message is still on. I'm scared, Sophie. If something happened to Ellie, my world would end."

Sophie tried to comfort him. "Maybe she and Lele got drunk or something."

"No. She only drinks now and again, but knows her limits. Why didn't she answer me?"

"Maybe her phone died?"

"Maybe. Please call Ben and see what he can find out."

"I will. Everything will be all right. We'll laugh when we find out it's nothing."

"I hope so."

"I'm going now. Remember I love you."

"Love you, too. Keep Ellie in your prayers."

It was three in the morning when Henry's phone rang, but it wasn't Ellie or Sophie. It was Kaitlin. The tone of her voice terrified him. She blurted out, "Henry, something happened to Ellie."

He felt Ellie, but it wasn't good. He sniffed hard. "What happened?"

"The police aren't sure. Neither Ellie nor Leleina showed up for work today. The police did a wellness check. Ellie's apartment was empty, but..." Kaitlin sobbed, "at Leleina's house, they found a brutal scene. They won't tell us anything else other than both girls are missing and they don't know if they're alive or not. Oh, Henry."

Henry sent prayers to heaven. *I feel you, Ellie. I'm coming.* His voice was firm. "She's alive. I feel her. I'm flying to Honolulu."

"Jeremy and Ben left for the airport fifteen minutes ago."

"Got it. Thanks for calling. If you hear anything else, let me know."

Henry called Sophie next. She was beside herself. Henry called his mother on the way to the airport. She was crushed.

His mobile rang. Margaret. "Mum just told me. I'm coming. I'll meet you there."

"No. Stay home. I'll call when I arrive."

"Like hell. Ellie needs us. I waited my entire life for a sister and God granted me the one I wanted. There's no way to keep me away. If you see her before I get there, tell her I love her."

It took Henry twenty-two hours to reach Honolulu. He'd called Kaitlin, but there was no news. She said Jeremy would meet him at the airport. True to her word, Jeremy and Ben were there when he cleared Security. The look on their faces chilled him to the bone.

Chapter 26

*T*he next two days were hell for Henry. No news. The police provided no information. Margaret arrived in Hawaii and lifted his courage. The feelings from Ellie were vague, but still there. *If it's the last thing I do, I promise I'll find you.*

His mobile rang. An unfamiliar number. "Hello."

"Henry? Henry Campbell?"

"Yes. Who is this?"

"I'm Cassandra, Ellie's mom. I'd like to talk to you, face to face."

His arms shook with anger. *After what you did to her? Witch.* "Why would you think I'd ever speak with you?"

"Please Henry. I want to..." He disconnected and immediately blocked her number.

Henry and Margaret shared a very cheap motel room. No one seemed to know what to do, but Henry and his sister took action. From five every morning until almost midnight, they stopped at any and every place they could find on Oahu, showing Ellie's photo around, but no one had seen her. Ben stopped by their room every night, bringing food. He seemed to need Henry for therapy.

"Do you feel her?"

"Yes."

"What's she feeling?"

"Confusion and darkness."

"Can she feel you, too?"

"I'd like to think so."

"Please tell her Sophie and I miss her, and love her."

Henry and Margaret tried to bolster each other's spirits, but Margaret cried herself to sleep every night. She feared the worst. But in his heart, Henry knew Ellie was alive.

On day five, Henry and Margaret walked into the street. That's where they saw them, papered on every pole. Robertson's picture was above the caption, 'Leleina lives — $25 Million reward for her safe return'.

"Maybe someone will find her... and Ellie."

"No one gives a damn that Ellie's missing, too. I swear to God, Margaret, I'll find her or die trying."

The next morning, a knock sounded on the door before they left. A uniformed police officer. "Morning. Are you Henry Campbell?"

Fear crept up Henry's spine. "I am. Do you have news about Ellie?"

"No, but I'd like you to come to the station with me."

"Why?"

"The detective wants to ask a few questions. Maybe you can help us find her."

Something didn't feel right. Margaret must have felt it, too. "I'll come with you," she said.

The officer turned to her. "You'll have to wait here. Someone will give Mr. Campbell a lift back."

Once they arrived at the police station, Henry was ushered into an interrogation room. A tired looking man entered the room.

"Thanks for coming in, Mr. Campbell. We need some background information on Ms. Lucia. How do you know her?"

"She's my fiancée. We met in London last summer."

"When was the last time you spoke with her?"

"The day before Valentine's Day. We skyped."

"What'd she say?"

"We talked about her day. She and her colleague were going to have a cookout on the beach."

"So they were having a party? Did she say if anyone else was coming?"

"I took it to be just the two of them. Why do you ask?"

"It looks like a party that went wrong."

Fear gripped Henry like a vise. "What do you mean, a party gone wrong?"

"Evidence of alcohol and... some other things."

"What other things?"

"I can't tell you."

Henry's ears perked up. "Why not?"

"Was she a party girl?"

The detective's inference wasn't lost on Henry. His face heated with anger. "No, she was... I mean... *is* a good girl. Only ever slept with two men."

"Really? You and who else?"

"Both were men from her distant past. We're waiting until we get married."

"You sure she didn't sleep around or like more than one guy at a time?"

Henry leapt from his chair. "You dirty-minded bastard. My Ellie's a good girl."

The detective placed his hands on Henry's chest. "Calm down. We're trying to understand what happened."

Henry buried his head in his hands. "Campbell, we researched your girlfriend."

"My fiancée."

"Fiancée. We found this website called 'EllieLucialovesto...'"

Henry jumped up a second time. "She didn't create that, that despicable thing. My ex-girlfriend made it to trash Ellie. She hacked Ellie's accounts."

"Who?"

"Her name's Heidi Fries. The London police can tell you all about her. She's rotting in some jail cell in England."

"For trashing Ms. Lucia?"

"When they investigated, they found other things she did. Contact the London police if you don't believe me."

The investigator made a sign at the mirror.

"Do you remember what Ms. Lucia was wearing that night?"

Henry closed his eyes tightly. "Yes."

Henry opened his eyes to two glossy colored pictures.

"Was she wearing either of these?"

Henry studied the photos. One was a torn navy blue dress. He barely recognized the second dress. It was the one she'd worn when he proposed, but it was shredded and had black splotches all over it.

When he realized the dark splotches were blood he nearly lost the contents of his stomach. It took all of his resolve not to cry. He pointed at Ellie's dress. "That hers."

***

Margaret was exhausted when she closed the door to the apartment. Twenty past eleven. She'd tried to contact Henry all day, but he didn't answer. She turned on the lights and jumped when she saw the silhouette.

Henry was sitting on the floor, head down. She knelt next to him. "Henry?"

"They lied to me."

"What?"

"They told me their investigation is no longer for a missing person. It's a murder investigation."

Her vision blurred as she held him. "I'm sorry, so sorry."

Henry stood and punched the wall. "Lazy idiots. She's alive. I feel her."

"Are you sure? Maybe they're right. Maybe it's..."

His face turned red with rage. "No! I'd bet my life she's alive. They're taking the easy way out. Bet they're still looking for the other girl, but Ellie's not important enough."

"She is to me. Tell me what to do."

Henry's eyes blazed. "Don't ever question what I feel. If you don't believe me, go back to Scotland and leave me alone."

***

The weeks slowly slipped by for Henry. Her family had a memorial service for her, but Henry refused to attend. Ben brought Ellie's mom to see him, but Henry slammed the door in her face. She'd hurt Ellie and he'd never forgive her. Ben stopped by a few nights later. His eyes were red.

"I'm heading back to Sophie tomorrow. Wish there was more I could have done. El... Ellie was such a special woman."

"She still is."

"How can you be so sure she's alive?"

Henry raised his chin. "We're one. I feel her, in my heart."

Ben wiped his arm over his eyes. "What do you feel?"

"Her love for me. Despair. Asking me to find her. And I will."

Ben shook his head and looked away. "Wish I had your faith."

"Give Sophie my best. Tell her how much I appreciate her daily calls."

"You're the brother she never had."

Henry sniffed. "Second closest friend, ever."

"Come visit us, when this is over."

"Ellie and I will."

Ben's lips trembled. "Kiss her for me."

"That I will."

"You're a great man, Henry Campbell. Godspeed."

Henry woke the next morning to the realization that he and Margaret were the only two people still looking for Ellie. The only two who believed she was still alive. He was so bitter. Ellie had been right on Thanksgiving night. Her real family didn't really care about her at all. But Henry was her family now. He and Margaret. Some bonds were more important than blood.

Their days and nights became an endless blend of walking, showing Ellie's picture, asking if anyone had seen her and getting negative responses. Money was tight. They only ate one meal a day. Henry worried about his sister. She'd always been slender, but he could easily see her bones. Margaret's mind was consumed with finding Ellie. Henry knew his sister worked harder at it than he did.

He woke Margaret up and offered a glass of water. "I'm worried about you. You should return to Scotland."

"Like hell, I will. I waited my entire life for a sister and I'll be damned to give up. Go back home. I'll never quit, not while there's any possibility she's alive."

Some days, Henry's spirit dropped so low, he began to doubt himself. Was what he felt coming from Ellie, or was his mind grasping for straws? But the feelings in his heart were so real, so strong. She had to be alive. Ellie missed him terribly and wanted him to rescue her. And he felt her love, undeniably. He fell asleep, exhausted, holding onto the necklace. *Henry love Ellie loves Henry.*

He knew she drew her strength from their love, just as he did.

***

Mid-March turned to mid-April. Margaret looked at her phone. April 17th. Ellie's birthday. The day Henry and Ellie were to wed. Ellie had asked Margaret to be a bridesmaid. *We'll find you. You'll make a beautiful bride.* She said her morning prayers and forced herself out of bed. The tap water tasted horrible. She walked into the next room. Henry sat staring out the window.

"Morning, Henry." The look on his face scared her.

"I want to tell you how blessed I am to have had you as a sister," he said. "It's time for you to go home. It's over."

Her whole body shook. "What happened?"

"Ellie gave up hope. She told me goodbye. I felt her ask me to meet her in paradise." Henry wiped his eyes. "This is the last day. If we don't find her today, I'll meet her there, tonight. Kiss Mum for me. Goodbye."

Henry kissed her forehead and walked out.

Margaret fell to the floor. She didn't understand the bond her brother and Ellie had, but she knew it was real. Something horrible must have happened. *Grant me strength. Help me find her.*

She followed her heart, tears in her eyes. *Watch over Henry.* Midmorning found Margaret walking down another endless street, hitting the ethnic grocery stores and bars with her photo of Ellie. Suddenly, an overwhelming urge to visit a specific location hit her. She followed her heart to Li's Pawn Shop. She'd been there numerous times and didn't have a clue why she felt compelled to go there now.

Outside the shop, her hope suddenly rose. She entered, not knowing why. She knew the man behind the counter. He was talking to a younger man with wild hair, a dark tan and ripped clothing. The man stunk. Margaret smelled dog feces and urine. She gasped when she saw the man pull a necklace from his pocket. The necklace was identical to the one Henry wore.

Margaret quickly stepped outside and called Henry's mobile.

"Yes?"

Her voice cracked. "Get here, now. There's a man in this pawn shop. He has Ellie's necklace."

Henry's reply was strong. "Are you sure?"

"Identical to the one around your neck. Hurry. I'll watch for him."

The man left the pawn shop and entered a bar down the block. A strong hand grabbed her arm. She screamed and jumped. But it was only Henry.

"Where is he?"

"In that pub. The pawn shop's right there."

"Keep an eye out for him. I'll get Ellie's necklace. Back in a jiffy."

"Hurry. Don't know how long he'll be."

Henry returned in less than five minutes. His expression frightened her.

"Did you get it?"

"Yes. Her engagement ring, too. Wait until I get my hands on that bastard. He'll be sorry."

The man stumbled out of the bar at one in the afternoon. Brother and sister followed him to a marina. The man climbed aboard a cabin cruiser. The name 'Wildest Dream' was painted on her bow.

Chapter 27

Ellie woke with a pounding headache. Her eyes finally focused. Alone, in a small room without windows, she could see that the concrete floor had a small cot with one pillow and a blanket. There was an open headed five-gallon bucket with a couple of rolls of toilet paper, a towel and several washcloths. Several jugs of water, some orange juice, snack crackers and fruit were in a corner. *Where am I?* She had no idea. She recalled the home invasion and her fight with the attackers. *Situational awareness.* Ellie had forgotten about the fourth attacker. He had slammed her head repeatedly against the mirror. Placing her hand on her forehead, she felt a bandage. Her left arm sported a second covering, in the same location the nurse had placed it when she gave blood.

The room smelled of dust. Glancing at her body, she realized these weren't her clothes. They were Lele's and they felt tight on her. She tried to stand but the room spun.

She fought off panic. "Is anyone there? I need to use the bathroom."

A female voice replied, "The bucket's your toilet. Drink the orange juice. It's still cold."

"Where am I?" No response. Her mouth was dry and tasted like she'd been chewing on rubber gloves. Ellie relieved herself in the bucket. She drank the juice and ate some crackers. Ellie took inventory of her condition. Her head pounded and she was dizzy, but otherwise appeared fine. Her next thought was of Henry. Instinctively, her hand grabbed her necklace. It was still there, as was her engagement ring.

The room was her world for several lonely weeks. Once a day, two men would enter, masks on their faces. They never spoke to her. One would hold a baseball bat as if he'd strike her if she got too close. But they didn't harm her. Every day, they'd replace the bucket and replenish her crackers and water. The room had no windows or lights. It was so dark. She was utterly alone. She spent her time walking the walls and talking to Henry in her mind. She felt his love. She knew he was searching for her.

Ellie replayed the memory of every second she'd spent with Henry. Every word, each kiss, the touch of his hand. She sang songs to him. She willed him to find her, imagining his lips on hers. That was the only thing that maintained her sanity. Ellie tried to come up with a plan of escape, but for the first nine weeks, no opportunity presented itself. She called out to Lele, but there was no answer.

The opportunity for escape came one morning. Only one man entered the room. He waved the baseball bat at her, but placed it on the floor while he replenished her supplies. Ellie acted swiftly. She grabbed her bucket.

The man caught her movement and reached for the bat but Ellie was quicker. She threw the bucket's contents in his face. He cursed her. She grabbed the bat, and struck him in the head. He went down like a ton of bricks and didn't move.

Guide my feet, God. The hallway outside was empty. Ellie locked him inside and tried to get her bearings. She considered searching for Lele, but that might cost her the chance for freedom. *I'll be back, with help.*

Sunlight poured in through a crack of an exterior door. The brightness almost blinded her. She threw open the door to the outside. Ellie ran into the sunlight for the first time in months. She was thankful she'd kept herself in shape. The ocean was a hundred yards away. To her right was a large house. Ellie ran left, taking a tiny trail through the jungle, until she came to a small secluded cove. Another island was within view, only a few miles away. There were houses there.

Ellie had no hope that her escape would go undetected. She planned to wait for the cover of night. She had passed a dog cage, so her captors would probably use animals to hunt for her. *How can I throw off their scent?* They would soon look for her. A dead log floated close to the shore. Ellie swam, but doubted she'd have the stamina to make it to the closest island. With the log to cling to, she might make it. She continued running to another cove. A small island was several hundred yards off shore. Making sure her footprints were evident on the beach, Ellie entered the water, but swam back to the cove where her log was waiting.

She hid under some palm fronds that touched the ocean. Before long, the search was on. Under her fronds, she watched as several men followed the dogs. They carried some sort of rifles, like soldiers. The dogs sniffed the log before following her trail around the island. Within half an hour, a large motorboat roared by. Ellie shrank beneath the waves. Just before dark, the boat passed Ellie again.

Night falls quickly in Hawaii. She waited for total darkness before retrieving the log. So far, her plan was working beautifully. At first it was difficult making headway against the waves, but fortunately, the tide started going out. Ellie held onto the log, kicking for all she was worth. She was making headway toward the closest island. Adrenaline fueled her effort, but then her legs cramped. It was painful, but still she persisted. The next island was drawing closer.

Suddenly, a spotlight lit up the water around her. She lost her grip on the log. The light went out. She was disoriented. Hands suddenly yanked her hair. Someone forced her under. No matter how she struggled, she couldn't surface. She'd tried to hold her breath, but couldn't do it. Her attacker was relentless. Sea water filled her mouth and throat. Her body jerked in spasms. Suddenly, her head was above the water. She saw the hull of a boat.

Strong arms pulled her from the ocean. She was thrown up onto the deck. Several men pounced on her, beating and kicking her. Ellie blacked out.

Cold water brought her back to consciousness. She was back in her room. A man appeared in the doorway. He stunk of urine. Must have been the man she'd hit with the baseball bat. He grabbed her by the throat, lifting her into the air before slamming her body against the wall. He punched her repeatedly before again throwing her to the floor. Jumping on top of her, he ripped open her shirt.

"You little bitch. That's the second time you hit me over the head. Think you're tough? I'll find a tender spot to make me feel better." He grabbed the top of her shorts.

Two men restrained him. "Leave her alone. She's our payday. We each get a hundred grand for her. You touch her and the boss will kill all of us. We've got orders. Don't touch the merchandise."

The man breathed heavily. "Wants to act like an animal? Put her in the dog cage. See how she likes that. The dogs'll sleep in here tonight." He drug Ellie to the dog kennel she'd passed. He stopped to kick her body every couple of yards. After the other man left with the dogs, he beat her unmercifully and threw her into the kennel. He yanked off her necklace and forcibly ripped the ring from her finger.

Ellie fought back, kicking his legs out from underneath him. He landed in dog feces. He cursed and hissed, "I'll be back tonight. Make it look like you escaped again. But you're coming with me." He told her what he had planned for her.

"Enjoy the hot sun today and think what I've got in store for you. You'll never see daylight again." He viciously punched her and she passed out.

***

Margaret watched the man board the *Wildest Dream*. He opened a beer, sat on a lawn chair, and placed his feet on the rail. She couldn't tell if he was sleeping or watching the marina. The boat yard was deserted.

In her ear, Henry whispered, "We need to get him below deck and set sail."

Margaret came up with a plan. Henry acted first, whistling as he strolled the dock. Margaret ripped the top of her tee-shirt to show her cleavage. She strolled the dock until she reached his boat. The man must have been sleeping because she hailed several times before he responded.

"Nice boat. What's the story behind the name?"

He removed his glasses and checked her out. He laughed. "Got me some wild dreams. Want to be part of one?"

Never. "Maybe. Like to get to know you first."

"Want to come aboard and get acquainted?"

She forced a smile. "Love to."

When he offered his hand, the stench almost made her throw up. Her skin crawled from his touch. He led her below decks, closing the door behind them. Margaret was checking the interior when he grabbed her hair and shoved her against the bulkhead. His fingers of one hand were tightly wound in her hair while he snaked the other hand under her shirt. The combination of stale beer and halitosis was overwhelming when he forced his mouth against hers. *Hurry, Henry.* His tongue was like sandpaper against her lips.

A burst of sunlight caught her eye. The man released his grip on her hair as he reached for the arm that choked him. Henry's arm. Her attacker struggled and tried to reach for leverage, but he was no match for Henry's fury. The man's arms fell limp at his side. Henry flung him to the floor. The look of murder covered Henry's face.

***

The heat made it difficult to breathe. Fencing blocked the trade winds. No shade, either. Ellie tried to focus, but was having trouble. She touched her lips, only to find dried blood caked there. She could tell it was split open. Her entire body was sore. The man's threat rolled into her mind. All hope was gone. *I won't make it.* She rubbed her eyes. Thoughts of Henry filled her. *I'd give anything to hold you one more time.* Her life was over. *No longer your future, but your past. Love you, Henry. Meet me someday in paradise.* The hot tropical sun broiled her skin. So thirsty, but the only water in the kennel was in the dog's water dish. *Take me home.* Her strength quickly faded under the relentless sun.

***

Margaret had never seen Henry so angry as when he found the man's trophy box. He'd searched through the photos several times. She knew he was searching for Ellie's picture. He finally threw the contents of the box into the corner. He grabbed a pail from a locker and went outside. He returned seconds later and threw the bucket of seawater into the man's face.

The man coughed and shook his head. He glanced at both of them. "Who the hell are you?"

Henry gripped the man's chin. "I'll do the asking." Henry held up Ellie's necklace. "Where did you get this?"

He spit in Henry's face. "Screw you."

Henry had a maniacal look in his eyes. "I'll ask you one more time before I get rough. Where'd you get the necklace?"

"I ain't telling you nothing, limey."

Henry stood. His fingers jerked in spastic movement. "I'm Scottish, not British. We're tougher, meaner. You had your chance to end this easily, but no. That's one approach to take."

Henry pulled off his shirt and threw it on a seat. He shot Margaret a look.

"Go outside and wait. Close the door and don't you dare come back in."

"What are you going to do?"

"There are things little sisters should never see their brothers do."

***

Something had woken Ellie. There it was again. A cool touch on her shoulder. She turned rapidly. A homely looking girl with curly red hair knelt next to her. Something was odd. The girl's image was almost transparent. The girl had an understanding smile on her face. "Hello, Ellie."

Am I seeing things? "Who are you?"

"I'm Annie, Henry's Annie. I have a message for you."

Ellie's skin tingled. *Finally gone over the edge.* "Sorry. Who are you again?"

The girl smiled as she gently touched Ellie's face. Her touch calmed Ellie. "I'm Annie. God has heard your prayers. I was sent with this message. *Don't lose faith.*

Henry's coming, He's well on his way. Be strong. And thank you for visiting my grave."

Ellie shook her head and squeezed her eyes shut. But when she opened them, the girl was still there. "You said we'd meet someday. Today is that day. I offer you peace, but more importantly, hope. It's almost over. Never, ever lose faith, for God loves you very much and He is with you. I must go, but I'll see you again someday. Peace be with you, my friend."

Ellie blinked her eyes and found herself alone in the kennel. Stars were beginning to light the sky. *I lost it. Miss you, Henry. I'll be waiting for you in paradise.*

Chapter 28

argaret focused her eyes on the horizon and blocked out the noise from below deck. She felt someone behind her. Henry. His skin glistened with sweat. He was breathing hard.

Henry pointed toward the edge of the ocean. "She's over there. About thirty miles."

Her heart almost leapt out of her chest. Hope beyond measure. "Are you sure? She's still alive?"

"Yes, but she'll be better when we get her off that wretched island. Here's the map he drew."

Margaret looked at the paper. There were stains on the map. Red stains. Margaret motioned toward the cabin. "He still breathing?"

Henry studied the map. "For now. Might need him later."

"What are we going to do?"

"We'll wend our way toward the island. We want to get there under the cover of dark. Then I'm going to get Ellie."

"I'm coming with you."

He cupped her chin and smiled. "You've done enough. You found the necklace. Ellie will be free, because of you."

His face suddenly screwed up. He sobbed hard and held her.

"How can I ever repay you?" he asked.

"Bring my sister home. It's time."

"I agree. When we get there, you'll stay on the boat. This will be dangerous."

Margaret pursed her lips. "We came this far together. I won't let you go alone."

"Suppose they kill me. Then what?"

She studied his eyes. *Always looked out for me. My turn now.* "Do you realize you've always been my hero? When you step foot on that island, I'll be there with you. If you die on that island, they'll have to bury us together."

***

Henry ran the last two miles without lights. A quarter mile off the beach, he cut the engines. Their captive said both Ellie and Leleina were imprisoned there. Henry dumped the man into the Zodiac raft tethered to the cabin cruiser. Quietly, so they didn't draw attention, they rowed the raft to the beach.

He checked his watch. "Twenty minutes until the guards change." The brute had revealed the guard's rotation and check-in schedule. After the shift change, he and Margaret would have thirty minutes before the next radio check.

Henry pushed the man out of the Zodiac and tied him to a palm just off the beach. He grabbed the man's throat. "If you've lied to me, God have mercy on you... because I won't. And just wait until your buddies find you here. Bet that'll be fun."

Henry and Margaret worked their way deep in the shadows, finding a secluded spot to wait for the changing of the guards.

***

Ellie knew her chances of survival were slim. The evil man had shared his plan, which would result in her eventual death, after he tired of using her. *If I only had a weapon.* Not much to work with. As she wracked her mind for a solution, a story Jeremy once told her awoke in her mind. Jeremy had been a Ranger, but one mission had gone horribly wrong. Weaponless, his pursuers were bent on capturing him. He told her how he'd sharpened a rock to defend himself.

The water dish came to mind. *Will this work?* She groped for it in the dark. Ceramic. Yes! She slammed it against the concrete floor until it shattered. She selected one long piece of the dish and rubbed it against the rough concrete. The man said he was coming. Ellie had a surprise waiting for him. One he'd never forget.

***

Henry watched the man and woman walk from the big house to the holding cell shed. They entered the building and thirty seconds later, the outgoing guards exited. As soon as the two entered the big house, Henry patted his sister's shoulder. Time for action. As quietly as possible, he opened the door. Voices rang out from a small alcove down the hallway. That would be the kitchen area. Margaret followed as he hugged the wall.

At the corner of the room, Henry whipped around the bend. The male had his back to Henry, but the female shouted a warning. Henry delivered a vicious backhand blow which sent her flying into the corner. The male guard stood, turned and reached for a holstered knife. Henry punched him in the head repeatedly, but the man grabbed Henry's arm and flipped him to the floor. He drilled his knee into Henry's chest while fingers dug into the flesh on Henry's neck. The knife suddenly appeared right over Henry's heart. *No!* Henry grasped the man's knife hand with both of his, trying to force it away. His peripheral vision caught the female guard pulling her knife, ready to join the fight.

The tip of the blade entered Henry's chest. The man was stronger than he'd anticipated. Another half inch and the fight would be over—just not how Henry had anticipated.

A loud yell drew his attacker's attention. Margaret appeared, swinging a wooden bat. She swatted the knife from the woman's hand and hit her squarely in the face. The female was out of action.

The man turned his head to glance at her at the same time his sister wound up. "Leave my brother alone!" she yelled.

Margaret struck as hard as she could. The snap told Henry she'd broken his arm. The man released the knife and tried to stand. Margaret finished him with a home run to the head. He hit the floor and ceased moving.

Margaret dropped the bat and fell to her knees. She cradled Henry in her arms. "Are you hurt? How bad did he cut you?"

He kissed her cheek. "You saved my life. With your big stick."

She laughed. "Nothing you wouldn't have done for me. How badly are you hurt?"

Henry stood. "I'm fine. We need to move." He searched the man and found the keys.

"Check the rooms. He said Ellie would either be here or in the... *kennel,*" he winced. "I'll take care of these two."

Henry locked the unconscious guards in a room.

Margaret yelled, "First five rooms are empty. Maybe he lied."

Henry ran down the hall. Ellie might still be here. He met Margaret at the last room. He threw open the door.

A beautiful Hawaiian girl trembled before his eyes. "Are you the police?"

Margaret replied, "No. We're Ellie's family. Here to rescue her."

***

Ellie's pain was non-stop. Henry's face floated before her sight. *Remember how the world faded away when we'd look into each other's eyes?* These were her last moments on earth. She'd never overcome that man's strength. *If only I could...* Noise. Footsteps. Coming toward her. This was it. *Tell Henry I love him. I'll be waiting in paradise.*

The rust of the chain link fence felt like sand against her fingers. The footsteps were closer. Ellie hoisted herself to her feet. Show time. Her appointment with destiny. She steadied herself with her left hand. In her right, she grasped the weapon. *Watch over Henry.* A light illuminated the lock. Hands inserted the key, stripped away the lock and yanked the gate open. *It's now or never.* The element of surprise was hers. Ellie lunged and wrapped her arm around her attacker's torso. With every ounce of her strength, she plunged her weapon deep into his mid-section and shoved it from side to side.

The man's body quivered. She ripped the knife from him and wound up, prepared to repeat her assault. Ellie smiled when the man grunted in pain. Before she could send the knife forward, the voice she loved with all her heart filled her ears. "Ellie, it's me. Henry. Here to take you home."

***

Henry touched the hole in his gut. A warm, sticky substance covered his fingers.

Trembling hands touched his cheeks. "I didn't know it was you. Forgive me. Love you so much. Are you hurt?"

His pain was sharp. A time and place for everything. *Ignore the pain. Focus on the mission. Not safe here.* The pain would have to wait. He grasped Ellie's face and touched his quivering lips against hers. Her tears wet his face.

"Ellie, I love you. Thank God you're alive. We need to get you out of here. Can you run?"

"N-no. I'm pretty dizzy. Escaped yesterday, but they caught me. Gave me the beating of my life."

"I'll carry you, but we must hurry. Freeing you was the simple part. Getting out of here alive'll be harder." Henry felt a groan leave his lips when he swept her up in his arms even though Ellie was so light.

"Henry, what are you..."

"Quiet. Not out of the woods yet. Gotta get you home." Henry headed into the jungle, but stumbled as he ran. Several times he fell, but quickly got back up. Ellie gripped his shoulder.

She screamed, "They're right behind us!"

He was so tired. "Shh. Margaret and Leleina... that's who are behind us. Gotta get to the Zodiac."

The inflatable boat was suddenly before him. He stumbled again. *No strength.* The wound was serious. His pants were soaked. Henry forced himself to focus. It took all his strength to lift Ellie into the boat.

Margaret ran up next to him. She helped Leleina climb in. Henry was gasping for air. The baying of dogs rent the night. *The race for freedom is on.* He and Margaret shared a quick look before shoving the boat off of the beach.

Margaret jumped in. Henry tried to, but missed. He floundered in the surf and hung onto the raft. *No energy.* Hands grabbed his shirt and arms, pulling him up and over the gunwales. He collapsed on the deck.

Margaret shook him. "You all right, Henry?"

Ellie answered, voice quivering, "I-I-I s-stabbed him by accident."

Margaret lit his mid-section with her flashlight. Her hand went to her mouth. "Oh my God."

Henry glanced at the sight. His pants and shirt were soaked with blood.

Margaret pointed the lamp at his face. "You're so pale."

He ripped the light from her hand. "Stick to the plan. We're sitting ducks here. Get us away from the beach."

Ellie tried to wrap her arms around him, but he pushed her away. "Not now. I've a job to do."

Margaret fired up the engine and steered the Zodiac to where the *Wildest Dream* drifted in the waves.

Ellie reached for the railing. Henry grabbed her, kissing her lips. "You stay with Margaret and never forget. I love you." Henry turned and reached for the rail. He tried to pull himself on board, but fell back into the Zodiac.

Margaret grabbed his shoulder. "Henry, I'm scared."

Everything was spinning. "Get me on that boat and get the hell out of here."

Margaret helped boost him onto the bigger boat. He tried to stand, but fell to one knee.

Then Margaret's face was next to him. "Godspeed. Such an honor... you as my sister. Get outta here."

***

Ellie didn't understand. Why did Henry get on the boat and make her stay in this, this raft? They belonged together. Margaret opened the throttle of the Zodiac, putting distance between them. Ellie's mouth dropped open when she looked back at the craft. Henry was up and moving.

Margaret turned and Ellie could no longer see Henry. The running lights on that boat flickered to life, lighting the sea around it. Before her eyes, it changed direction, away from them. The lights became little pinpoints in the darkness.

Ellie fell backwards when Margaret shut down the engines. The night was silent, except for the soft sound of waves kissing the raft and the horrible sound of his sister's sobs. Ellie reached for Margaret. The two held each other tightly.

Leleina's arms warmly encircled both of them. "I can't believe we're free, Ellie."

Ellie's eyes searched the horizon. Henry's feelings filled her chest. Love. Devotion. And something else. Her mind tried to comprehend what it was as the lights of the *Wildest Dream* grew smaller and smaller on the horizon.

Chapter 29

Precious little time remained. Henry turned the marine radio to the channel the Coast Guard monitored. His hands shook as he keyed the mic. "Mayday, Mayday, Mayday. Hailing the U.S. Coast Guard. Do you hear me?"

A deep voice responded. "This is the United States Coast Guard. Identify yourself and state your emergency."

"This is the motor vessel *Wildest Dream*. Two miles south, southeast of Wayward Island. I found the two kidnapped girls. Need immediate medical attention. Armed kidnappers in hot pursuit. Help us, please."

A brief pause ensued before a second voice came on. "Repeat your transmission. Did you say you have two kidnap victims on board?"

Everything was getting fuzzy to Henry. He was shaking uncontrollably. Looking aft, he saw bright lights from another boat following him. The gap between them was probably just three miles. "Ellie Lucia and Leleina Robertson. On board. Kidnappers in hot pursuit. Need assistance immediately. They'll overtake us soon. When we hear the helo, we'll send up flares. Follow the flares!"

"*Wildest Dream*, you hold on. Help's on the way."

The exertion took almost all his energy. Henry held onto the bridge chair. "Hurry... I'm seriously injured... don't know... how long... I'll be conscious."

"10-4, stand-by."

***

Ellie shivered in the ocean breeze, despite the blankets Margaret wrapped around her. Henry was in pain. Bad pain. Though small on the horizon, she could pick out his boat. A second set of lights appeared some distance behind him. Ellie grabbed Henry's sister's arm. "Look, help's arrived."

"I don't think so. It's too soon. Those are probably the people who imprisoned you. Henry suspected this would happen."

The stars overhead were so bright. "Then why would he..." Her hand went to her mouth. "He's the bait, isn't he?"

Margaret sniffed hard. "Yes."

"That's why you took us away from him. Why he turned all the lights on."

Margaret sobbed. "To draw them away from you. 'Til help gets here."

"Is help coming?"

"I hope so. I pray to God he sent out the SOS."

***

The USCG cutter, *Daniel Printz*, was forty-eight nautical miles away. On the bridge, Captain Livingston barked his orders, "General quarters. All full ahead. Light up the chopper. Fire team and corpsman on board." He walked and stood behind his radar man. "Can you pick them up? Any vessels that can assist?"

The radar operator pointed. "This must be him. Second larger vessel is less than three nautical miles, same course and closing. Two large ships within twenty miles, by their size, container ships. Wait! See this sir?"

Livingston did. He yelled another order, "Hail that ship, now."

***

The gap continued to dwindle. Henry had jammed the throttle full ahead. They'd taken the bait. He needed to draw them away while not getting too far away from the Zodiac. The effort to maintain consciousness was harder than he'd imagined. The bridge chair was slick. From his blood. So tired. Not much time. *Where the hell are they?* Ellie was so close to freedom. *Love you, Ellie. Knew you were alive.* He needed sleep. So tempting to close his eyes, forget the pain. Henry slapped his face and muttered, "I'll sleep when I'm dead."

***

The destroyer, *USN David Farragut*, was the other ship. Lieutenant Walker received the call from the Coast Guard and immediately took action.

"Wake the captain. Sound battle stations. Get the UAV airborne. Flank speed and set a course to intercept that boat."

The ship vibrated noticeably as the engines pushed her full throttle. The propellers bit deep in the ocean and the destroyer heeled hard to port. Claxons and screamed orders added to the cacophony as the ship came to life, preparing for combat.

The captain burst onto the bridge. "Sit rep!"

Livingston brought him up to speed.

The captain nodded. "Well done, lieutenant."

"Sir, images from the UAV."

The captain's face grew red. "Kidnappers, hell. They're pirates. Not on my watch. Show them these waters belong to the United States Navy."

***

The gap between *Wildest Dream* and her pursuer was less than a mile and closing rapidly. Much faster than Henry had anticipated. *Where the hell's the Coast Guard?* He needed to stay in the vicinity, but keep his pursuers away from the Zodiac. If they found the raft, all his effort would be in vain. So he spun the tiller, making a sharp starboard turn as if to head toward the closest island, some six miles distant.

He gulped in the sea air as he turned to glimpse aft. Bad move. He'd reduced the approach angle, allowing his pursuers to gain on him. Henry needed to stall for more time. He threw the tiller hard to port before straightening out the bow. He keyed the handset and screamed, "Coast Guard. This is *Wildest Dream*. They're about to board us. Are you coming? They'll kill all of us."

The glass windscreen shattered as bullets destroyed it. Henry's left arm exploded from a direct hit. He screamed into the radio, "We're taking fire, automatic weapons! I'm hit. Help!"

"Hang in there, son. Help's coming. Eight minutes out."

To avoid the incoming fire, Henry dropped to the deck. It'd be over in less than five. He'd failed. When they boarded, they'd kill him. They'd quickly find the Zodiac... and the girls. *I need a miracle.*

It was impossible to outrun the others. He had to stay the course. Suddenly, a massive explosion ripped the water apart five hundred yards ahead. *Naval artillery?* The kidnappers had overshot *Wildest Dream* and evasively turned to port. Directly in front of Henry. He should turn to match their course, but instead, he kept *Wildest Dream* pointing dead ahead.

The violent collision threw Henry down the ladder into the galley. Water was rushing in. The hull had been split. Despite his exhaustion, Henry smiled. God had given him the miracle, allowing time for help to arrive. Henry crawled to the stern rail. Everything grew dim. His engines were still at full throttle, even as the deck settled closer to the ocean surface.

The thud alerted him. *Wildest Dream* was being boarded. He'd been a marine, a sailor. The endless sea. *My last home. I love you, Ellie. Goodbye.* Henry rolled over the railing into the ocean.

As soon as he hit the water, he knew his life was over. No flotation device, no strength to push himself to the surface. The curtain was closing on his final act. His life flashed before his eyes. One thing stood out. *Ellie's love.* Her spirit had been with him, forever.

The water was dark. Ellie would be safe now. Calmness came over him. *Grant her peace, love and happiness. Tell her I love her.*

Suddenly, something warm touched his hand. Henry's eyes flew open. *Annie?* His Annie, right in front of him. She said with urgency, "Don't give up. Ellie needs you. Your future's ahead of you. I've held your sons and daughters in my arms. Girls with dark black hair and brown eyes, like Ellie. Sons with green eyes and reddish brown hair, just like you. Kick, Henry, kick! All of Heaven's with you."

Henry blinked his eyes, but Annie was gone. His exhaustion was complete, yet suddenly, strength beyond measure welled in his legs. Henry kicked violently, breaking the surface of the water.

A voice screamed, "There he is! Shoot that son of a bitch."

Time stood still. The engines on *Wildest Dream* were silent. To his left, the whisk of a helicopter could be heard approaching. To his right, a throbbing, as of powerful engines. Then brilliant, sudden illuminance lit the sky to his left.

Margaret had fulfilled her duties. Two additional flares followed, lighting the sea. Despite his pain, he smiled. Success. He'd once promised Ellie he'd gladly lay down his life if it meant saving hers. Today he'd made good on that promise. *I'm ready, Lord.*

The gunmen had stopped momentarily to watch the flares in the distance. As one, they pointed their assault rifles at Henry. *Goodbye, Ellie.* Henry was at peace with his world and with God.

Violent bright light cut a swath through the night. Henry was pushed aside as a wave rolled over him. Then a massive gray wall appeared on his right.

A deep voice boomed through the night, "This is the United States Navy. Drop your weapons immediately."

One of the gunmen squeezed off a round at the hull of the ship. His mistake brought an immediate response. A wall of fire and lead eliminated Henry's attackers.

Henry looked toward the ship, but the bright lights blinded him. A harsh voice screamed, "Cease fire!"

His mind was foggy, his vision dim. The adrenaline was gone. No energy. She was safe now. *Love you, Ellie. For eternity.* Ellie's face was the last thing he saw. Henry sank beneath the surface of the Pacific Ocean one final time.

Chapter 30

Ellie's teeth chattered as she watched it unfold. The rhythmic burst of automatic weapon fire brought her heart to her throat. A sudden dirty yellow flash blinded her, followed by the noise of the explosion. *Henry!* She finally understood this. It was all to protect her. Yet she couldn't understand his feelings. The calmness. The peace. Serenity.

Several things happened in brief succession. Toward the horizon, brilliant white lights interrupted the night. The sound of a helicopter. Margaret jumped into action, taking hold of a yellow device that looked like a toy gun and firing. A flare lit the sky. Twice more she shot, sending flares overhead. Then, a brief thunderous clap like thunder. Pain seared across Ellie's chest, as if someone had ripped her heart out. She could no longer feel Henry. Ellie fell to her knees and her vision blurred. *No, please. Don't take Henry.* Two pair of arms wrapped around her.

The thump-thump-thump noise drew closer as droplets of water stung her face. *You can't be gone.* Her heart and mind probed the distant night, searching for Henry's feeling. Nothing. The pain in her chest grew. Her mind went back to that night in her room, when he'd told her what his love meant. *How can I go on without you?*

The three women were rapidly hoisted on board the aircraft. She no longer cared. Someone wrapped blankets around her, but it did little to stop the jerky movements of her limbs. A man examined her. He rubbed something on her split lip before applying a bandage.

Henry's face was before her and her mind replayed memories. The little things they'd said, or done, or felt. Someone handed her a cold bottle of water, instructing her to drink it in sips. Ellie had lost track of time, but the helicopter banked sharply to the left. Some order was apparently given, as the four armed men started organizing the gear near the door. Ellie became aware of Margaret. Henry's sister sat by her side, tightly holding her hand. Her cheeks were wet. Ellie touched her face. Margaret threw her arms around Ellie.

A thud rumbled through the chopper. The men sprang into sudden action, quickly handing things out the door. Strong arms guided her to where other men waited to lift her onto the deck of a large ship. Ellie thought the men were sailors. The girls were shepherded against the rail. Downdraft blew up a corner of a tarpaulin, exposing three sets of blood-covered legs.

She cried out, "Henry!"

Quick movement caught her attention. A team of men ran with a lone stretcher to the chopper, rapidly securing it to the deck. Ellie recognized the man on the stretcher. Henry! She tried to run to him, but the sailors restrained her. The doors slammed shut and the chopper quickly rotated off into the night.

***

Margaret was horrified. The sailors reassured her that her brother had been alive when they whisked him off. But Ellie and Henry had some special connection, some indescribable bond. Ellie didn't respond to anything. Ellie had felt it. Henry was dead.

Margaret's mind drifted back to her childhood. As a little girl, she'd been terrified of storms. When thunder shook their house, she would run to Henry's room. He'd held her until the storm had passed. She felt his arms comfort her now. *Everything will be all right.*

All of them had been assessed for injuries. Margaret and Lele were fine, but the sight of Ellie's bruised and battered body was horrible. Welts, cuts and bruises covered the majority of her skin. *Poor Ellie.* The girl stared blankly ahead when they examined her. When they were done, a blanket was wrapped around Ellie. Sailors led them to a shower room. The water was warm as Margaret washed Ellie's filthy, bruised body. Ellie didn't respond, blinking without seeing.

After the shower, Margaret helped her dress in clothes the sailors had provided. They were shown to a cabin. She helped Ellie into a berth. Ellie's eyes were vacant, blank. Margaret sat next to her, holding her hand. The exertion of the night and swaying of the ship rocked Margaret into a deep but troubled sleep.

***

Ellie tried to close her eyes, but Henry's face haunted her. From the moment they'd met on the dock until his final actions earlier, he'd shown nothing but love. *And now he's gone.* Was life even worth living anymore? Margaret had been a rock, doing things Ellie couldn't. Kind, gentle, just like her brother was. *Had been.* Margaret had passed out from exhaustion, neck bent at a weird angle as she sat in the chair.

While Ellie watched her sleep, she suddenly became aware of two other figures standing in the room. Both were dressed in white and almost transparent. It was Annie—Henry's Annie. She smiled sweetly at Ellie and touched her face. Ellie's skin tingled where Annie touched her. She moved aside and a man took her place.

She knew exactly who he was. He looked like Henry, only older. Henry's father now stood before her. He smiled and kissed her forehead. "Sleep in peace, my daughter. You're safe now." He turned to Margaret and kissed her head. "My little girl. I love you, Maggot." Ellie blinked her eyes and they were gone. *Have I gone insane?*

Margaret jumped from her sleep. "Popsie, are you here?" Margaret's breath came in clumps. She forced herself to breath calmly. Margaret stroked Ellie's hair. "Sorry. Dreamed my pop was here."

Ellie stared into her eyes. Campbell eyes, a reflection of Henry's. She whispered, "He was here. I saw him kiss your forehead. He told you he loved you and called you Maggot."

Margaret's face blanched. "Maggot? Are you sure?"

Ellie nodded.

Margaret's eyes filled with tears. "That was his nickname for me."

Ellie reached for her. The two held each other tightly. Ellie no longer knew what to say or do.

***

Six thousand miles farther east, Sophie rubbed the dirt from her hands. *Ellie.* She missed her best friend so much. She'd planted pink hyacinths around the remains of the stone house Ellie had bought. The fragrance of the flowers surrounded her. She drew her knees to her chest and had a good cry. Where was Ellie? What was she going through? Was she even alive anymore?

Sophie wiped her cheeks with the heel of her hand. Would she ever see Ellie again? Sophie and Benjy spent many hours praying for their friend. But Benjy had given up hope two weeks ago. So deeply depressed. Sophie tried hard to raise his spirits, but nothing worked. So she murmured a long prayer for Ellie and Benjy.

Later she walked into the kitchen, wiping her cheeks with dirt-covered hands. Eleven fifty-five, close enough to eat lunch. Ben had left for Chicago the previous evening. She scrubbed the dirt from her hands and fixed herself a sandwich. Sophie turned on the television to catch the noon news. The plate fell to the floor, breaking into dozens of pieces.

***

Kaitlin walked into the staff meeting where her husband Jeremy, John Stange and several other managers waited with forlorn expressions. Since the disappearance of both Ellie and Leleina, the mood in the office had been subdued. Laughter used to ring in the halls frequently, but tears were now the norm. A memorial for the two missing women filled the entire lobby.

Kaitlin was briefing the team on a new project. While she waited for her presentation to upload, Ben's ringtone sounded. Poor Ben. He'd taken it so hard. Kaitlin suspected he still loved Ellie. Jeremy had confided in her that one of the reasons Ben had been called to Chicago was so John Stange and Jeremy could talk to him. They wanted him to take some time off. Ben's depression seemed to hang in the room. She saw Ben shove his phone in his pocket.

"Morning, everyone. Today I'm..."

A different tone now rang from Ben's phone. Kaitlin stopped and waited for him.

Ben reddened. "Sorry. I'll silence..."

Ben's hand flew to his mouth and tears formed. Tingles crawled up Kaitlin's spine.

"Are you okay, Ben?"

He stood and ran to her. He was trembling all over. He handed her his phone. "Read the text. Out loud."

She read it silently first. *Oh my God!* Now she was shaking. Kaitlin passed the phone to Jeremy.

Jeremy also read it. He coughed to clear his throat. "The text is from Sophie, Ben's wife. It reads, 'Ellie's alive! Rescued in Hawaii. Story leading the news. Heading to Honolulu to be with her. God answered our prayers.'"

Pandemonium broke out. There were no dry eyes in this room.

***

Cassandra Lucia sat alone in her kitchen. Her eyes roamed through the chairs of the big kitchen table, remembering fun times when her children were home. When she'd had six children, not five. Moments when she and John were still whole and in love. Today was it. The last time she'd call this place home.

She sat in the chair Ellie used to occupy. Her family's intervention on Thanksgiving Eve had opened her eyes. She was the one to blame, not Ellie. She was the one who'd had too much to drink. The one who slept with her brother-in-law. The one who got pregnant to someone other than her husband. All her life Cassandra had been tough on Ellie, but she'd severely persecuted her daughter after her husband John found out. Ellie, the young girl who made simple, honest mistakes. The one who was such an easy target for ridicule and blame.

For a second she could hear her firstborn laughing with abandon over some corny joke. That memory brought a smile. She could also see her daughter's devastation that night. *Told her I regretted her birth.* How could she have been so stupid and cruel? When her eyes were finally opened and Cassandra tried to make it right, it was too late. And now Ellie was dead. *I'd give anything for one last chance... to tell you how much I love you.* Yesterday would have been Ellie's twenty-seventh birthday, but that sweet little girl with the twin dimples was gone.

Fifteen minutes of drunken lust shared with her husband John's brother twenty-eight years ago had finally destroyed her life and her family's happiness. Her husband had only stayed because he didn't want to lose all he'd worked so hard for.

She gently touched a picture of her children from a family vacation, finger hovering on Ellie's face. Her bitterness had hurt her daughter. It was too late to make a difference for Ellie, but she could still make one for John. She'd no longer stand in the way of his happiness. Earlier, Cassandra had given her resignation, effective immediately. She was leaving John. In three hours, she would board a plane for Chicago, where her parents and sisters would help scratch together a new reality. Life in Savannah was over.

The memory of John's strong arms stirred other memories. Happy ones. Magical times. Cassie didn't want to tell him in person, so she'd texted him. She wouldn't contest it. He could keep everything except a small savings account and her retirement. This was it. The lowest moment of her life.

She drank a quick glass of wine to bolster her strength. The cab would arrive any second now. She had just loaded the empty glass into the dishwasher when her phone rang. Kaitlin. *Not now.* Cassandra couldn't deal with her sister at this moment. She silenced her phone.

Cassandra jumped when the kitchen door flew open. John. He was out of breath and his eyes were red.

"I just got your text. You're leaving me? How could you?"

Her cell rang again. Kaitlin. She sent it to voicemail. Cassandra turned to him. "I ruined our lives. I blamed our daughter for something that was my fault. We should be holding her, but our precious baby girl is dead."

"Cassie, she might still be alive. That boy believes she is."

Her tears fell, puddling on the floor. "Our baby's dead, John. We have to face the facts. She isn't coming home. Our love's dead, too. I know the reason you've stayed. It wasn't love." She touched his face. *For the last time.* "I'm sorry. I hope in time you'll forgive me. I... I love you. Gonna go now. I know the way out." She turned and the cellular device sounded again. "Damn you, Katie." She silenced it once more.

The warm hand touching her arm surprised her. He turned her to face him, then embraced her. His voice was uneven. "Don't go. I know what you think, but I hung around because I loved you. I waited all this time to hear you ask for my forgiveness. That's all I ever wanted."

She stared at him in disbelief as he pushed her long hair from her eyes.

"I will forgive you on one condition. If you forgive me for wasting all these years. Please."

John kissed her lips, for the first time in forever. His kiss broke the dam. Tears both of joy and sorrow hit the floor. Nothing had ever felt better. His arms were wrapped tightly around her.

A new noise sounded on both their devices. John read Jeremy's text out loud, 'John, Cassie, this is URGENT!!!!! Please, please, please call Katie ASAP! URGENT. Need to talk to you NOW!'

"Oh God. Something must have happened to your parents. Call her back, Cassie. I'll be right by your side. Forever."

***

Sophie sat at the gate waiting to board the flight to Honolulu. Her bottled tea was weak, and she wished it were stronger. Glancing at the television monitor, a ship filled the screen. Scrolling across the bottom was a caption, 'Live feed from Hawaii'. She ran to the monitor so she could hear the commentary.

"We're coming to you live from Honolulu." A pretty Hawaiian girl ran down the gangway to the waiting arms of a very large man sporting a white Stetson. "That's Leleina Robertson, heir to the Pearl of the Pacific fruit empire. She's being reunited with her father."

The camera panned back to the gangway. Two girls clung to each other as they departed the ship. The cameraman zoomed in on their faces. Margaret was crying as she led Ellie. Sophie's skin turned cold when she got a look at Ellie's eyes. They were blank. *Where's Henry?*

"The two women are Eleanor Lucia and one of her rescuers. We're getting reports a second rescuer was gravely injured and airlifted to Honolulu. Reports are sketchy as to whether he survived."

Sophie threw her hands over her ears. "No, no, no!" People around her started to move away. There must be some mistake. He was her best friend. She needed him. Henry couldn't be gone.

Chapter 31

Margaret saw them at the bottom of the gangway. Police. The officer was apologetic. "Ladies, we'd like to ask a few questions."

Ellie shook her head. "I just want to go home."

"Won't take but a few minutes. I'll drive you."

She and Ellie were separated. Margaret was scared this would be a difficult interview, but she was wrong. They listened to her story, asked her to write it down and then told her to wait until Ellie was finished.

The afternoon was turning into evening. The door to the waiting room burst open. Sophie.

Sophie enveloped Margaret in her arms. "Where's Henry?"

The room was blurry. Margaret bit her lip. "Pretty sure he didn't make it."

Sophie's eyes moistened. "Please no. Are you sure?"

"I am," Ellie's voice came from behind them. "Henry sacrificed his life to save me."

Margaret whipped around. Ellie had entered while she was talking to Sophie.

Ellie stood like a statue, staring at her friend. "I'll have to live with that. Every day."

Sophie was inconsolable. She fell to her knees and Margaret tried to comfort her. Ellie didn't move.

A uniformed officer entered and removed his hat when he noted the angst in the room. He gently tapped Ellie's shoulder. "Miss Lucia? I've been told to take you wherever you want to go. Can I take you to the hospital?"

Ellie nodded her head. "I'd like that. I want to see his body one last time."

"Did you say 'body'?"

"Yes. Henry Campbell's body."

"Umm..."

Ellie blankly stared ahead. "Yes. He died saving me."

"Who told you that?"

"No one. I know. I feel it in my heart."

"Might need to get your heart looked at. I was told he just cleared surgery. Alive."

**

Ellie wondered if her feet even touched the ground. *Henry's alive!* She still didn't feel him inside, but who cared. A nurse escorted Ellie into the care unit. She wasn't prepared. Henry lay in a hospital bed, tubes and wires attached all over his body. His left arm was bandaged from the shoulder down. His color was pale. More covering across his chest and stomach, with hoses disappearing into his abdomen. Henry's eyes were closed. *Never thought I'd see you alive again.* What hell had he gone through for her? Ellie held his good hand, kissing it as she told him over and over again how much she loved him.

Henry's eyes opened. Immediately, a tired smile lit his face. His words were slurred, "Ellie, s'good t'see you, my love. Have I told you today how much I love ya?" She nodded because she couldn't speak. "Happy birthsday, honey."

She fought back tears as she spoke. "I love you so much. I feared I might not ever see you again. Didn't mean to stab you. Wish I could undo it. Can you forgive me?"

He tried to wink at her but his motor skills weren't quite there yet. "Yesp. You'se all right? Why's you has bandages on your lisps?" The words were coming out, but were hard to understand. "Are syou hurt?"

"A little, but that doesn't matter. I'm just so glad to see you." Ellie could no longer hold back the tears of joy as she kissed his hand. "Are you in much pain?"

She could tell he was tiring. "You's all rights. So beautifuls ta me."

Ellie thought how she must look. Her body was covered in bruises and welts, her eyes were both black. She had an ugly bandage on her lip and was desperately in need of a haircut.

Then it happened! For the first time all day, Ellie could feel Henry in her heart. Feelings so wonderful. Henry's love was once again coming in loud and strong. They talked for a while, until a nurse came in to check him.

"He needs his rest. Looks like you might need some, too."

Henry dozed off. The nurse told her she'd bring in a cot. Ellie couldn't wait to tell Margaret and Sophie about Henry.

Ellie returned to where Sophie and Margaret sat in the waiting room. They hugged her, asking about Henry. They ate in the hospital cafeteria, Ellie's first real food in weeks. Then they went to visit Henry. He was fast asleep.

Margaret knelt and kissed his cheek, thanking God for saving her big brother. Sophie pressed her lips to his forehead. Her bright red lipstick left lip marks there. Sophie reached for the tissue box, but stopped when Ellie laughed.

Sophie was puzzled. "What's so funny?"

"Don't wipe it away. I'll pick on him about it later."

As the three sat there, Ellie thought how Henry had touched each of their lives. *Such a good man, my man.*

An hour later, Henry awakened. His words were clearer. "Can a man get some food here? I'm famished."

Ellie giggled. "I'll call for the nurse." She pulled the call bell and a knock immediately came to the door. "That was quick."

But it wasn't a nurse. It was Leleina and a giant of a man. He held a white Stetson in his hands. Leleina gripped Ellie in a warm embrace. Leleina looked absolutely radiant.

Henry asked, "What's going on?"

Ellie answered, "You have a visitor. Henry, meet Leleina."

Leleina interrupted. "We've met. Both your fiancé and his sister. This is my dad, Duke Robertson."

"So honored to meet you, Henry Campbell." He turned to Henry's sister and extended his hand. "So you are the heroic Margaret Campbell. Truly an honor to meet the both of you." His eyes swept over both of them. "I'm forever in your debt for rescuing Lele. You could simply have left her there. If you did, I know I never would have seen her again."

Ellie's heart swelled with pride for both of them. Margaret held Henry's hand. "My brother's taught me a great deal in life. The greatest lessons were love and honor. Couldn't have lived with ourselves if we'd left her behind."

Duke bit his lip. "I can never thank you enough."

Leleina hugged her father. Robertson smiled and wiped his cheeks. "That's why I consider you two to be heroes. Heroes deserve to be rewarded, usually with ticker tape parades. But I think I have something better. There's the small matter of the reward. Both of you earned it, so both of you get it."

Ellie felt Henry's words before he spoke them. Humility. "We couldn't accept. We were only doing the right thing."

"And I am, too. I won't take no for an answer." He handed Ellie and Margaret business cards. "I know things are crazy right now, but after they calm down, call me. I'll personally arrange the transfer. It was so nice to meet you. Oh, and if you ever need anything, you call me. I can get heaven and earth moved. Goodbye."

The door closed. Margaret grabbed Ellie's hand. "This means we're filthy rich."

Henry shook his head. "No, Margaret. It just means you're filthy. Get a shower."

Ellie laughed when Margaret pinched his nose.

"Filthy, my foot. It means I can buy the house next to you, no matter where you go."

Henry gave Ellie a crazed look. "Well, there goes the neighborhood."

***

Ellie told Sophie and Margaret to head to a hotel. She was staying with Henry. After visiting hours, a nurse came in and removed Henry's IV. Ellie waited until she left before doing something against hospital policy. Ellie crawled into the hospital bed with Henry. The warmth of his arm was wonderful, but paled in comparison to the feelings from his heart. He held her tightly as she snuggled against his chest, ever careful not to touch him near his wounds. No words were spoken or needed. For the first time since November, they both slept soundly.

Ellie was deep in her favorite dream. Walking through an evergreen forest, breathing in the delicious scent of pines. Next to her, holding her hand tightly was her love, her Henry. They paused at an overlook, looking down on a valley that had a river running through it. Starlight and moonlight glistened off the water's surface.

Henry's lips sought and found the mark of her lips. Suddenly the moonlight dimmed as dark clouds rolled in. Ellie forced herself to wake.

Henry's feelings were coming to her, a combination of both fear and anger. She glanced at his face. His eyes were fixated toward the foot of the bed. She suddenly turned and couldn't believe who stood there in the hospital room. Her mother and father!

Ellie was astounded. "Mom, Dad, is that really you?"

Her mother reached for her as Ellie slid out of bed. Cassandra whimpered, "Oh my baby. I love you so much, Ellie."

Her father embraced them both. His shoulders trembled as he sobbed.

Ellie felt Henry. Worry. Skepticism. Hate. Ellie knew it was because of how her mother had treated her.

Ellie wriggled free. "Mom, Dad, so glad to see you. I missed you."

Her mother kept touching her face. "We thought we'd never see you again, but you're alive. This is truly a miracle."

Ellie pulled away, holding her mother's hands. "Mom, I had a lot of time to think about it while I was in captivity. I don't know what I did to make you mad all those years ago, but whatever it was, I apologize. I hate this thing between us. Is there any way we can work it out?"

Her mother wiped her eyes. "You never did anything wrong. It was me, all me. I need to beg for your forgiveness. But first, I need to thank Henry for saving you." Cassandra kissed Ellie's forehead and turned to Henry. "Henry Campbell, I'm sorry for treating you the way I did. I'd like to start over, okay?"

Henry stared at her. Distrust. Caution, for Ellie. He nodded his head, but still frowned.

Cassandra whispered, "Thank you." She placed her hand over his. "I'm Ellie's mother, Cassandra Elizabeth Lucia, but you can call me Mom. Thank you, so, so much for saving Ellie. I, uh..." Ellie stared in disbelief as her mother wrapped her arms around her fiancé, crying on his shoulder. She kept muttering, "Thank you, thank you so much, Henry."

Ellie's dad waited his turn. "I'm John Lucia, but I'd be honored if you'd call me Dad. I regret not taking your hand when you offered it before Thanksgiving. Please forgive me."

Henry didn't say anything. Ellie knew he was analyzing them, their intentions. He studied Ellie's face. His demeanor softened as he felt Ellie's spirit lift.

Henry cleared his throat. "Now that we're on somewhat friendly terms, I have something to say." He paused and studied their reactions. "Mr. and Mrs. Lucia, your daughter and I plan to be wed. I'm hopelessly and forever in love with her. I'd appreciate your blessing over our marriage. Will you give it?"

Ellie hoped they would give their blessing, but wasn't prepared for the reaction. Cassandra threw her arms around him, kissing his cheeks as she called him her son. John pumped his hand repeatedly. They responded together. "Yes, yes, yes!"

Epilogue

*T*he smell of fresh cut grass filled everything. Henry couldn't believe the changes that had occurred in the last four months. The old run down house looked like a mansion. The newly built 'celebration' barn sat across the drive. The beautiful gazebo where he would wed his Ellie was picturesque. And the landscaping? Flawless.

Ben handed him a water bottle. "Gonna be a hot one. Keep hydrated."

Henry was speechless. So many blessings he and Ellie shared. But their love was the sweetest one. *Ellie, love you so much.*

His younger brother Harry tapped at the door. The man of many words muttered, "Time."

The guests had all arrived, Henry and Ben walked to the gazebo. Henry stopped to kiss his mother and Ellie's grandmother, Nora. Everyone laughed when Ellie's aunts Martina, Kaitlin and Kelly stood and reached for him with open arms.

He took his place in front of the pastor. To his left stood Ben, the best male friend he had ever had in the world. Ben, now his nextdoor neighbor.

The front door to the house opened. Sophie gave Ben and Henry the thumbs up. *Time to marry my best friend.*

The Navy band filled the air with sweet music. Kaitlin's twins, Megan and Kelli, spread pink rose petals behind them. Jeremy Junior carried the wedding rings. The bridesmaids processed. Anticipation filled the air as everyone waited for Ellie to make her grand entrance. Then the band music stopped.

Henry's heart leapt when he caught sight of her. Her heart was full. Love. Joy. Bliss. Sophie and Margaret both fussed over the bride's train once she was outside.

Ellie looked at him. As if magic, everything else faded. Memories, their story passed back and forth between them. The night they met. The picnic at Diana's. The first kiss. Paris. The proposal at Longwood. And now, their story was continuing in front of their eyes.

Ben broke the spell when he patted Henry's shoulder. "We've both been blessed, Henry, very blessed."

Henry couldn't take his eyes from Ellie. "She looks like an angel, doesn't she?" Ben nodded.

Ellie's parents were waiting on the porch for her. Ellie had asked both of them to walk her down the aisle. Henry saw her dad softly kiss her hand. He saw Cassandra lift the veil and kiss her daughter. Then Ellie wrapped her arms around her mother.

John Lucia nodded to the U.S. Navy captain who directed the band. Smiling, the leader tapped his baton to get the musicians' attention. The wedding song began and Ellie and her parents processed. Margaret and Sophie followed along, still fussing over her long train.

Henry could feel her love pouring to him. Such wonderful feelings. He sought and found her eyes. A humorous exchange took place in their minds. Impulsively, they ran to each other. She leapt into his arms, kissing his lips feverishly. "I'm sorry. Couldn't wait any longer to hold you. Love you so much."

He worked his kisses up and down her neck. "You're my dream come true. I couldn't wait either. I love you forever and ever."

Once again, it happened. The world slowly faded away until there was nothing but two sets of eyes, two sets of lips. Their lips touched again and they whispered into each other's ears at the same time. "Forever!"

Peals of laughter wildly echoed through the crowd. The pastor walked forward, clearing his throat. He spoke loud enough for everyone to hear. "I know you're busy sharing a moment of solitude, but I was wondering, would you two like to get married today? I mean, the guests are here. Food's ready. It'd be a perfect time, you know? Just saying..."

They nodded, but Henry grabbed Ellie one last time, giving her a kiss that drew cheers from the crowd.

They somehow behaved, barely getting through the vows. When it came time for Henry to kiss his bride, Ellie threw her arms around his neck and Henry wrapped his around her waist. Their lips pressed together once more, softly, but passionately. To their surprise, the band started counting out loud, reaching seventy-eight before the newly married couple broke off their kiss. They had to stop before passing out from lack of oxygen. Taking a deep breath, they picked up where they had started. Again, the world faded away as they held each other. It didn't matter that two hundred plus people were there to see the wedding. All that mattered was they were now one, officially and forever.

It took almost an hour to greet their guests. They held hands, slowly walking into the barn. As soon as they sat down, Ben offered a toast. Even though everyone was there, no one mattered but the two of them. Henry came out of the trance when Ben made a comment that Henry had better listen to Ellie or she just might stab him again.

Henry held Ellie and called to Ben, "Please get your story straight. She didn't stab me, she was marking her territory."

Ellie held her hands over her mouth as she giggled.

The night passed rapidly. It seemed only a few seconds had passed before the band played 'Moonlight Serenade'. Henry's mind drifted back to that first night, their first kiss. As she had done in London, Ellie softly sang to him. Henry gazed into her beautiful eyes, smiling when those twin dimples came out. His life was complete.

Romance appeared to be in the air for the wedding party. Margaret danced quite a few times with Ellie's brother Kevin. Edmund had been coupled with Leleina, but it was Ben's sister Tara who drew his attention. Harry also danced with Tara, three times. Henry noted the way Harry gazed into Tara's eyes.

Sophie was ecstatic to be there sharing the celebration with her two best friends. She had way too much to drink, but fortunately she waited patiently for her turn to dance with Henry. As they danced, she said, "I'm so happy for you two. Think of how far we've come. A short year ago, we were waiting for life to begin. And it happened. Both of us found the loves of our lives, didn't we?" Sophie's face was wet with tears.

Henry smiled at his friend. "Have I ever thanked you for introducing Ellie to me?"

Sophie looked a little wistful to Henry. "No. So glad you found happiness. I care about you. You know that, don't you?"

"Of course, Sophie, I do. After Ellie, you're the best friend I ever had. I love you, my dear." He smiled at her.

Sophie suddenly kissed him deeply on the lips. Her voice came in rapid bursts. "I need to clear the air between us. I need to know something. Before Benjy and Ellie came along, why didn't you and I ever become a couple? You had to know how deeply I was in love with you."

Henry felt a cold chill run up his spine. "Are you drunk, Sophie? Please tell me you and Benjy aren't having problems, are you?" He could feel Ellie's curiosity.

"I'm sorry. Shouldn't have brought it up. Just forget it."

Sophie and Henry stopped dancing as they stared at each other. Henry was aware Ellie was watching them intently. They turned to face her simultaneously.

Ellie eyed the pair. "Hi, guys. What's going on here?"

Sophie blushed. "Just telling your husband I thought he was wonderful, that's all." She kissed Henry's cheek before turning to Ellie. "And you, you're the luckiest woman in the world, ever." She hugged Ellie before leaving the bride and groom standing in the middle of the dance floor, staring at each other. Fear filled Henry's mind.

Ellie smiled as she reached for Henry's hand. "Let's dance, sweetheart." She watched Sophie leave. "Finally told you, didn't she?"

Henry was very confused and becoming more concerned by the second. "Ellie, I'm shocked at what she said. She said..."

Ellie kissed him. "Henry Thomas Campbell, don't you worry. I felt your confusion, your fear. Sophie told you she was in love with you before Benjy came along, didn't she?"

He stopped dancing as he stared at her. "How'd you know?"

"Keep dancing with me, sweetheart." She drew him close, "Remember when I stayed with her after William attacked her? She shared a lot of things with me that day. One was her confession she'd been in love with you."

Henry's hands shook. "Ellie, you have to believe me that..."

Again, she kissed him. "Henry, it's all right. When she told me, I was worried. We were just beginning. I didn't want to lose you. But I had to know the truth. I asked if you were in love with her and you said no. I believed you, Henry. And that hasn't changed. Know why?" Henry shook his head. "No one knows you better than I do. I have nothing to worry about. You've proven it time and again through your actions. I wondered if she would ever tell you. Piss poor timing on her part, I think, but since she's drunk, we'll forgive her."

She kissed him again. "Don't you worry about what she said, one bit. I'm not going to. Henry, I love you and I know you love me, with all your heart. We are one."

"It was pretty inconsiderate of her. It is our wedding day."

Ellie giggled. "You're so cute when you get mad. Please don't be upset with her. Enough about Sophie. May I change the subject, my darling husband?"

He was relieved. "You don't know how wonderful it feels to hear you call me your husband. Ask me anything you desire." When she smiled at him, those dimples he loved came out. He teased her. "And the answer to anything you ask will be yes!"

Ellie roared her head back, laughing at him. She kissed his cheek. "Keep that in mind for later tonight, okay? Henry, you still haven't told me where you are taking me for our honeymoon. You do realize, now that we are married and stuff, there can be no secrets between us. Spill the beans."

Henry's face brightened. "Let's see how well you know me. I will give you a hint. You once told me you wanted to visit this place, but didn't want to squander any memories by going there without me."

Ellie's eyes blazed as she blurted out, "Venice! Are you taking me to Venice?"

"Yes. We're going to Venice."

Ellie grasped him, kissing his lips ferociously. A drunken Italian voice interrupted. "Excuse me, love birds! Woo hoo! Yes, you two making out in the middle of the dance floor. Point your attention up her for a second." Ellie and Henry were both blushing. "Saw you two making out, you need to get a room. Margaret and I have yours prepared."

Sophie's voice turned serious. "Ellie and Henry, I know you two waited a long, long time for this day to come. There were many struggles. I wish you eternal happiness. I can't imagine how hard it must have been to hold out, to keep your hands off each other for so long and not to make love before today, but..."

Henry yelled at her. "Sophia Elena Miller! Be quiet. Don't go blabbing our secrets to everyone."

Sophie laughed. "It's all right, Henry. I wanted to tell you Ellie has a subliminal message for you in this next song." She turned to the Captain. "Maestro, let her rip!" Laughter filled the air as the captain turned to the band, starting them on Glenn Miller's 'In the Mood'."

Ellie grasped Henry tightly. "Patience. She may be drunk, but she hit it right on. You're getting lucky tonight. I waited my entire life for you." She reached up, and softly kissed him.

The rest of the evening was the stuff of fairy tales. All too soon, the guests left until only the immediate family remained. One by one, they bid everyone goodnight.

Henry swept his bride into his arms, and yelled over his shoulder, "Ta-ta and 'night, everyone." Henry carried Ellie into the house, up the stairs and toward their bedroom, only to find Margaret and Sophie blocking their path. The two had been in charge of designing their love nest.

Sophie whispered. "We need two more minutes."

Ellie laughed. "If it takes longer, we'll use another room. Might not be able to wait that long." Their lips blended together.

It was closer to five minutes before Margaret opened the door "All right, love birds. It's time to enter paradise."

Henry carried his wife into the room. Sophie and Margaret had outdone themselves. The walls were a soft pastel pink, the woodwork antique white. The furniture was a beautiful dark oak. The big four-poster bed sported a canopy of white lace with embroidered entwined hearts. "Moonlight Serenade" was playing softly across dozens of speakers, setting the mood.

The piece de resistance were the low intensity LED lights above the bed. The Celtic infinity symbol was surrounded by a ring of travelling LEDs that spelled, 'Henry loves Ellie loves Henry loves Ellie' in a continuous loop. The floor and bedspread were covered with thousands of rose petals. Hundreds of candles lit the room. Henry gently set his wife down on the bed.

Sophie and Margaret backed from the room. Margaret said, "Love both of you. Enjoy."

Finally alone, Henry stared into his wife's eyes. The world faded away. The love between them was magical. Ellie touched his face. "Henry, is this what forever feels like?"

Henry smiled at his love and touched those lips that tasted like honey. "Yes. We've finally arrived in paradise. I love you, forever and always, Ellie." He smiled and kissed his wife.

The End

Other Books by this Author

Seeking Forever (Book 1)

Kaitlin Jenkins is selected to embark on a six-month work project, out of her comfort zone and far away from her support network. If only she hadn't been assigned such a distractingly handsome partner—a former Army Ranger.

Jeremy is making his first foray into the civilian world. But he was not prepared to spend half a year on the road with a woman who seems even more heartless than his ex-wife.

Can love overcome the misunderstandings between them and the challenges of life on the road?

Seeking Happiness (Book 2)

Kelly lives a happy life. A great marriage, four wonderful kids and a fulfilling job managing an emergency department in L.A. But the day after her sister's wedding, her husband breaks the news. He is leaving her for Hollywood's hottest young actress and Kelly's world crumbles.

Then she meets the man of her dreams – smart, cute and romantic. The love of her life. And that's when the trouble really begins. Will she fill the hole in her heart? Will she ever find happiness and love again?

Seeking Eternity (Book 3)

 One bright September day long ago, Stanley Jenkins told his best friend, "See that girl? I'm going to marry her someday." Stan and Nora Thomas became best friends – soulmates – and fell in love. But when she told him she was engaged, he walked out of her life so she could find happiness. The loss was devastating.

Years later, when a waitress asks, "Stan, is that really you?" he looks up into the beautiful eyes of Nora, the girl he still loves. She's been widowed by her first husband, however Stan sadly notices the engagement ring on her hand. Once again, they become best friends... but as her wedding day approaches, is the cycle doomed to repeat?

Coming Soon

Whispers in Paradise (Paradise Book 1)

Henry Campbell's brothers are as different as can be. Harry is a quiet introvert who prefers to show his feelings through his actions. His family calls him the "man of many words" as a joke because he always uses the fewest words possible.

Edmund Campbell is gregarious, witty, overly touchy and a real troublemaker. When his older brother Harry falls in love with Tara, Edmund decides to steal her away. But when Edmund realizes he has actually fallen in love, he does something impulsive that affects the lives of the entire family.

About the Author

Chas Williamson is a life-long Pennsylvanian. Over his life, he has been many things: husband, father, grandfather, amateur historian, as well as a story teller. The desire to write started at a very early age. For years, storytelling was only verbal, but in 2013, a work crisis was looming as his employer of 30-plus years decided to close. His wife encouraged him to use writing as an outlet to reduce stress. When he balked, she asked him to write a short love story. That story grew into what would later become *Seeking Forever*. It continued to blossom into three other books of the Seeking Series and then a second series. The characters he has created are very real to him, like real life friends and he hopes they become just as real to you.

Made in the USA
Lexington, KY
27 September 2018